J. T. Fernie is the pen name of Moira Macfarlane. Her love of telling stories led her first into a career in teaching, then as HMI with the former Scottish Office Education Department. In 2001, she moved to Italy as British Consul in Florence, a post she held for eight years until retiring for the first time. Three years later, she took over as Acting Director of the British Institute of Florence for fourteen months.

Moira returned to Scotland in 2013 and lives in Haddington. She continues to travel widely and the books she writes draw on her experience of other countries and cultures. *The Istanbul Legacy* is her third book, following the success of *The Istanbul Ring*, published in January 2024, and *The Istanbul Gambit*, published in February 2025.

This book is dedicated to my brother, George Graham Robertson, who died in New Zealand in May 2016. I have used the first three intriguing pages of a book he intended to write but was unable to continue, to underpin the main story of *The Istanbul Legacy*. I hope he would have approved.

In memory of Edward Stewart, former rector of the High School of Dundee, who inspired my love of language and history.

J.T. Fernie

THE ISTANBUL LEGACY

For Mary – the very best of friends.

With my best wishes

Moira (J.T. Fernie)

AUSTIN MACAULEY PUBLISHERS®
LONDON · CAMBRIDGE · NEW YORK · SHARJAH

Copyright © J.T. Fernie 2025

The right of J.T. Fernie to be identified as author of this work has been asserted by the author in accordance with sections 77 and 78 of the Copyright, Designs and Patents Act 1988.

All rights reserved. No part of this publication may be reproduced, stored in a retrieval system, or transmitted in any form or by any means, electronic, mechanical, photocopying, recording, or otherwise, without the prior permission of the publishers.

Any person who commits any unauthorised act in relation to this publication may be liable to criminal prosecution and civil claims for damages.

This is a work of fiction. Names, characters, businesses, places, events, locales, and incidents are either the products of the author's imagination or used in a fictitious manner. Any resemblance to actual persons, living or dead, or actual events is purely coincidental.

A CIP catalogue record for this title is available from the British Library.

ISBN 9781037111778 (Paperback)
ISBN 9781037111785 (ePub e-book)

www.austinmacauley.com

First Published 2025
Austin Macauley Publishers Ltd®
1 Canada Square
Canary Wharf
London
E14 5AA

I am very grateful to my family: Mike and Jetinder, Helen and Euan, Sarah and Steve for their constant encouragement; to Skye for her ten-year-old wisdom; to Noah and Jemma for their quiet support; and to Toby who would like to create a TV series based on my books. Special thanks to Jetinder, for close-reading the text and for her constructive ideas on the plotline.

I am also very grateful for the support of two wonderful groups of friends: 'The Sunday Scientists' who have insisted on making a guest appearance in this book; and to Garleton Singers, the brilliant choir I am privileged to sing with, who insist on featuring in the next book. Thanks to the Scottish Arts Club in Edinburgh and to Haddington Library for hosting the launch of my books.

As ever, I am indebted to the staff at Austin Macauley Publishers for their prompt acceptance of my third novel. I am grateful for the advice I have received from staff in the production and graphics departments. Inspiration for this book has come from many sources, from security services at home and elsewhere; from my brother Graham who worked abroad for many years; from time spent in Istanbul and Sydney; and from research.

Finally, to my sister-in-law, Cathy, who finally tracked down the box containing the text my brother had written, which forms the prologue to this novel.

Table of Contents

Principal Characters	11
Prologue London April 2015	14
London A Few Days Earlier	17
Chapter 1: Istanbul January 2016	24
Chapter 2: At Sarnic Restaurant	33
Chapter 3: Istanbul	39
Chapter 4: An Apartment in Fatih, Istanbul	46
Chapter 5: Villa Demercaol	54
Chapter 6: Argentina 2010	65
Chapter 7: Berlin 2016	79
Chapter 8: Dinner in Berlin	83
Chapter 9: Schloss Stauffensee	86
Chapter 10: Sydney, Australia Five Months Later	90
Chapter 11: Fenez, Istanbul	101
Chapter 12: Dinner at Glebe Point Road	106
Chapter 13: Istanbul	112

Chapter 14: Istanbul 36 Hours Later	**118**
Chapter15: The Australian Outback	**123**
Chapter 16: The Toxteth Bar, Sydney	**141**
Chapter 17: The Search	**144**
Chapter 18: The Shangri-La Hotel, Sydney Twenty-Four Hours Later	**159**
Chapter 19: Aftermath	**164**

Principal Characters

In England and Istanbul
James Davidson: MI6 agent

In England, Istanbul and Australia
John Arbuthnot: retired superintendent, Lothian and Borders Police (now Police Scotland)
Anya Arbuthnot
Kadir Demercol: Commander, Istanbul Serious Crimes Directorate
Ayşe Demercol
Anoushka Demercol

In Argentina, Europe and Australia
Jens Timmerman
Jan-Marten Timmerman
Maria-Silvia Martinez
Grazia Timmerman
Fr. Federico Alvarez S J: Jesuit priest

In Istanbul
Harry Haversham-Hopkiss: ex-investment banker; long-term expat.

William Simpson: former MI6 agent—recently deceased
Ester Kalik: senior MIT agent (Turkish Intelligence Service)

In Europe
Descendants of Hans Peter von Seidel, war criminal
Magdalena Brandt: niece of Hans Peter
Dietrich Brandt-Stollenberg: great-nephew

In Australia
Robert and Mary Blyth: owners of a house once belonging to
Eileen Harriman: former MI6 agent—recently deceased
Anoushka Demercol
Jens Timmerman
Amos: a petty criminal turned kidnapper

E gli alberi voltarono
ancora per l'ascia
perché l'ascia era furba.
E li aveva convinti
che era una di loro
perché aveva
il manico di legno.

Italian translation of a Turkish proverb

And the trees turn
once more towards the axe
because the axe was devious.
And had convinced them
that it was one of them
because it had
a wooden handle.

English translation from the Italian. Moira Macfarlane.

Prologue
London April 2015

"Why on earth did you resign, James? Why, after so many years working your way up the ladder? You must have been in line for the top job when the DG finally retires to spend more time with his memoirs."

The remnants of an enjoyable dinner were strewn across the dimly lit dining table, trails of candle wax spilling in Kafkaesque patterns down the sides of polished candlesticks. The only other lighting in the room came from low Murano glass wall-brackets.

I turned to study the shadowy features of my life-long friend, Peter Jamieson, trying to work out what lay behind his question. Was it concern or disapproval? Apart from my ex-wife, with whom I remained on reasonably good terms, Peter and Helen Jamieson were the only people who knew where I worked though not what I did.

In answer to my continuing silence, Peter continued, "It's going to be very difficult for you to find anything interesting and challenging to do at your age, given your somewhat 'specialised' professional experience."

"What Peter means to say, James, is that we don't know what has brought this on, and we are worried about you." I looked over at Helen. The wall lamps cast a faint halo around her head, accentuating the concern written all over her face. "An exemplary career spanning twenty-five years with the Intelligence Services is a lot to walk away from. Is there more to this than a simple case of mid-life crisis?"

Why had I 'resigned'? How to explain complicated facts and conflicting emotions that you barely understand yourself? How to contain suppressed anger and hurt that threaten to surface like a powerful spring tide?

I had not resigned, I had been sidelined, given an assignment which took me out of the running for promotion, an assignment that I could not even tell my ex-wife or children about. I was to trace the footsteps of a man who may well have died for whatever it was he found out. I was to be on my own without backup. Biting down mounting waves of resentment, I took a mouthful of cold coffee in the hope that it might steady the turmoil in my head.

"I stopped believing," I replied, coughing to clear my throat and buy time. "I simply lost respect for the system and values I spent all these years upholding. Besides, if I am completely honest, it was not entirely a free choice."

"What do you mean?" Peter's voice was hesitant.

"I'm afraid there is no short and simple explanation," I replied.

"Well, we have as long as it takes," Helen said. "If you wish to tell us, that is. It might help, you know."

"In that case, let's leave the table and move to the lounge where we can be more comfortable. I'd better make more coffee as this could take some time."

"How much will you be able to tell us—or should you tell us?" Peter asked, rising from the table.

"Always the lawyer, Peter." I laughed. "But you have a point. There are a lot of things I shouldn't tell you. Well, all of it really, but as you are both upstanding members of the legal profession, I can always claim client confidentiality and, in any case, I really don't give a monkey's anymore."

How much could I tell them? I had an overwhelming urge to tell someone about what was happening to me, but that was impossible. Not even to a trusted friend I had known since childhood. I used the time it took to make coffee to conjure up an explanation for my imminent disappearance.

London
A Few Days Earlier

The strident ring of the telephone broke into my thoughts as I tried to compose the concluding sentence of a tricky case summary. It could only be the Director General at this late hour. Reaching for the receiver in exasperation, I lost my train of thought completely.

"Davidson."

"Ah, glad I caught you Davidson," the director's voice boomed down the line. "Thought you might still be here. Would you be kind enough to step upstairs. Something potentially serious has come up."

As usual, the DG did not wait for a reply and cut the connection immediately. Sighing, I looked at the unfinished report again, but the flow had gone. "Dammit!" I muttered rising to my feet in the required response to a summons from 'God'.

The corridors, in their customary décor of institutional green—*is there a factory somewhere that dedicates its entire production to green paint for government offices?*—were empty, and the elderly lift came almost immediately which was not entirely surprising given the lateness of the hour. Emerging from the lift into the corridors of power—or mahogany row, as we lesser mortals called it—I entered the DG's inner sanctum to find the ever-faithful Miss, not Ms, Porter guarding his door with her customary ferocity. She would have had Kharon[1] out of a job if she had lived in Ancient Greece.

"Evening," I muttered, still angry at the interruption, and with the prospect of dinner fading fast.

"The director is expecting you," she informed me, needlessly. "And you should be aware that he has an important engagement at ten this evening and will have to leave in little over an hour."

As if it would be my fault should his wife or mistress be inconvenienced by my loquacity!

The DG was standing near the window, looking out onto a typically dark, wet October evening.

"I hate London at this time of year," he said, without turning around. "Strangely, when you look back over the years, you seem to remember only good weather, not evenings like this."

He continued to stare out of the window for a few moments, before straightening up and returning to his chair behind the great mahogany desk.

"Sorry," he apologised. "Must be getting old. Please help yourself to a drink and make yourself comfortable."

When I was seated, he leant back in his chair and placed his hands flat on the desk.

"I appreciate that it is late and that you will be keen to get home, so I will come straight to the point.

---

[1] *Kharon was the feared boatman who ferried souls across the River Styx to Hades.*

"Within the last forty-eight hours, I have received reports of the deaths of two former colleagues, William Simpson in Istanbul and Eileen Harriman in Sydney. For the moment, neither death is being treated as suspicious, just unexplained. Given that they were in their late 70s, their deaths would have been unremarkable had it not been for the fact that both had been senior intelligence officers in this service; and both left the service in 1993 for undisclosed reasons—possibly connected to their work on the long-term fallout from the Cambridge spy scandal[2] of the sixties (not MI5's finest hour); and the belated disclosure in 1979 of the cover-up of Sir Anthony Blunt's involvement. Although they lived thousands of miles apart, Simpson and Harriman had apparently remained in contact.

"I was recruited to MI6 in 1979 to find that the usual schadenfreude on our side of the river at news of blunders by MI5 was muted by a sense that we, too, might have missed a few tricks regarding espionage activities linked to the Five in Türkiye and Russia.

"When I joined the service, Bill Simpson and Eileen Harriman were widely respected, experienced intelligence agents. While I did not get to know either of them well, Eileen was helpful to me in my early years. These were difficult times for both Intelligence Services. The disclosure that the Establishment had kept Anthony Blunt's involvement with the Cambridge Five secret for 15 years to avoid further embarrassment; and the wrongful suspicion that a senior

---

[2] *The Cambridge Five: Guy Burgess, Kim Philby, Donald MacLean, John Cairncross, and Anthony Blunt were Cold War double agents.*

officer in MI5, had been a soviet agent meant that the spotlight was on both services. Questions about our relevance and effectiveness were being asked in the House.

"Whitehall has never liked the fact that Intelligence Services sit outside its direct sphere of influence and was quick to exploit the situation to its advantage. As you know, it immediately changed policy regarding appointments to senior positions in MI5 and MI6 and, for several years, departmental heads were drawn from the ranks of Whitehall mandarins. The upside of this policy was that Whitehall was less likely to be embarrassed by public revelations of uncomfortable truths. The obvious downside of this policy was that these sensitive posts were held by people with little experience or understanding of intelligence work. By 1992, the policy had been dropped and the DG, Sir Evelyn Grimshaw, was a career officer appointed on the grounds of outstanding ability and in-depth knowledge of intelligence work. It was he who set up the special project on which Simpson and Harriman were engaged.

"Perhaps he was unaware of Simpson's obsession with trying to find out what exactly Kim Philby had been up to in Istanbul when he assigned him to the project, but if he had begun to suspect that Simpson was turning an official assignment into a personal crusade, that might well have been what precipitated the abrupt 'resignation' of both agents.

"Simpson had always suspected there was more to Kim Philby's operation in Istanbul than just the Volkov affair[3].

---

[3] *Konstantin Volkov was a Russian agent based in Istanbul who wanted to defect to Britain. He was betrayed to the Russians by Philby.*

Simpson claimed that there had been another Establishment cover-up, involving a high-profile individual who, according to Simpson, had been active in Istanbul long after the original spy scandal had become yesterday's news."

"Another Anthony Blunt, you mean?"

"Allegedly so. Getting back to the present—as you know, the deaths of all current and former operatives must be reported to this office without delay to ensure that no potentially embarrassing papers or diaries emerge from the deceased's estate; nothing that might contravene the Official Secrets Act. Colleagues confirm that Harriman's house in Sydney is clear and that, as far as they have been able to establish, she did not own a safety deposit box elsewhere or leave files with her lawyer.

"We are having more difficulty checking what Simpson may have left behind though. His flat is clear, but he often stayed with one or other of two women with whom he was in some sort of relationship. We believe that one of these women, Ester Kalik, worked—may still work—for MIT (*Milli Istihbarat Teşkilati)*, the Turkish Intelligence Service. The other woman is the cultural attaché at the Russian Consulate General in Istanbul. Getting clandestine access to their work or private premises will not be so simple.

"We have, of course, checked the archived personnel and operational files for Simpson and Harriman. The personnel files are complete, with relevant details of their respective careers up to June 1993 when they left the service. Significantly, these files give no reason for their departure. Their operational files record the specific projects and operations on which they were engaged up to August 1992. There are no operational files for the period from September

1992 to June 1993. The question is, where are these files, and why are they missing?

"As I mentioned, it was Sir Evelyn Grimshaw who selected Bill Simpson, Eileen Harriman and a researcher, George Tasker, to work on the special, top-secret project. I do not know what that project was. All I know is that the operational files relating to it are missing; Simpson and Harriman left suddenly in June 1993 and died unexpectedly a few days ago on opposite sides of the world. George Tasker died in a car accident in 1994. Sir Evelyn developed early-onset Alzheimer disease in the mid-90s and took early retirement. So, there is no one left who can shed any light on what that project was, or what risk it might have posed to those engaged on it. Or what risks it might still pose and to whom.

"In 1993, I was attached to the British Embassy in Washington, liaising with the CIA who still had lingering doubts about the extent to which they could trust British Intelligence Services. I was not privy to the facts surrounding the sudden departure of Simpson and Harriman, but the in-house gossip was that they had been pushed. Our American cousins greeted this news with concern as Bill Simpson was one of the few MI6 contacts they felt they could trust. They believed he was onto something, and their interest in whatever that was could well have sent waves of traumatic stress disorder along the corridors of power in Whitehall. Best to stop a British operative going rogue thereby helping the Americans uncover secrets better left secret.

"Bill Simpson left immediately for Istanbul, his obsessive desire to unmask a 'sixth man' undiminished. Eileen found it hard to adjust to life on 'civvy street', eventually choosing to start a new life in Australia. She remained friendly with Bill but did not share his obsession."

"This is all very interesting, Sir," I said with an eye on the clock, "but I am not sure why you are telling me all this."

"I want you to go to Istanbul, Davidson. Officially, you will have resigned for personal reasons. Unofficially, you will be working for us. I want you to go to Istanbul and bury whatever you find—permanently!"

G. Graham Robertson
Wellington
New Zealand 2002

Chapter 1
Istanbul January 2016

James Davidson stepped out of his cab at the address he had been given in Fatih Bey Cadesi to be met by an icy blast which he was sure must have come straight from the Mongolian Steppes. Istanbul—the fabled 'city of the world's desires'—was blanketed in freezing fog as daylight faded. Ethereal glimpses of the distant dome and minarets of the Suleymaniye Mosque shimmered through the gloom lending an otherworldly quality to the evening call to prayer. Standing outside the early 20th-century apartment block that was to be his home for the foreseeable future, James double-checked the address and looked around for someone to appear with keys.

A young man, dicing with death as he wove his way through the evening traffic, waved frantically as he approached James brandishing a set of keys and stammering words of welcome and apology. The main door opened onto a surprisingly large hall with a marble floor and tiled walls. An elderly lift laboured creakily upwards, depositing James and his luggage on the second floor, where he was met by an out-of-breath young property agent who had elected to climb the stairs—an option James decided he would take, for reasons of self-preservation, on all future occasions.

The apartment was larger than he had expected and comprised an attractive drawing room with floor-to-ceiling windows looking out over a balcony to a small garden. Large, hand-crafted wooden furniture was arranged around the room. Heavy tasselled drapes adorned the windows and ornate brass light fittings hung from the ceiling. The expression 'faded grandeur' crossed his mind. A dining room with a table that would easily seat 12 people led off from the drawing room—a pity, he thought, that entertaining was not going to be a priority on this mission. The kitchen was spotlessly clean although some of the appliances would not have been out of place in a museum. Three double bedrooms led off along an angled corridor as did a bathroom fitted with the largest bath James had ever seen, ornate taps, and a massive over-bath showerhead with Niagara Falls potential. The venerable WC and washbasin proudly bore the name of Shanks—home from home for an exhausted Scotsman.

When the anxious young property agent eventually left, having exhausted his store of useful information about the house and its environs, James threw himself onto a sofa to loud complaints from the venerable springs. He was too tired to unpack, too tired to explore the legendary delights of the local supermarket—if his young acquaintance's description was to be believed—and too tired to find a restaurant. The sheer size of the apartment accentuated his loneliness and his sense of being an intruder in a space where a family had once gathered, where friends had congregated for meals around the long table, where children had played on and fought over the venerable rocking horse in the corner.

Although he was single again—his ex-wife having tired of his frequent, unexplained absences which had an unhappy knack of coinciding with important family events—in London he never needed to be alone. He had friends, his club, access time with his teenage children, the gym, theatres and bars to take the edge off loneliness. In Istanbul, he had no one and his crash course in Turkish had left him well short of proficiency in the language, which would make engaging with locals difficult. The only date in his diary was a dinner the following evening at the residence of the British Consul General—in the residence rather than the Consulate because of his now ambivalent status in MI6.

*

After a day wandering around to get his bearings, James regretted that he wasn't in Istanbul as a tourist with time to enjoy the city, and all too soon had to return to his apartment to freshen up for dinner with the Consul General. Like all novices to Istanbul, he fell into the trap of an overpriced taxi journey to the residence, where he was met by a young Turkish man wearing a tailored suit, crisp white Nehru-style shirt and an engaging smile. In an elegant book-lined study, Tim Smith, the British Consul General, rose from his seat, arm outstretched, and welcomed him to the city. The CG was in his forties, well-built and tanned with a smile that reached his eyes and a quizzical expression on his face.

"I was told you were coming, James—if I may? Something to do with the death of Bill Simpson, a former MI6 officer, I believe. Now, before you tell me what all this is about, what can I offer you to drink?"

"A gin and tonic would be wonderful, thank you. I may not have much opportunity to drink my favourite tipple while I am here."

"True—there are hotel bars where you can find it, but Turkish wine is good and more readily available."

"Do you know if there were any suspicions surrounding Simpson's death?"

"You mean, whether he died of natural causes or not? I checked with our consular section in preparation for our meeting and they told me the death certificate records cardiac arrest as the cause. He was seventy-five and had not taken very good care of himself from all accounts, so I guess it wasn't unexpected. The only slightly unusual thing was that the last place he was seen alive was at the house of Ester Kalik who works for MIT, the Turkish Intelligence Service. I understand that Kalik and he were occasional lovers but kept separate houses. His body was found at the edge of wasteground not far from where Kalik lives. According to the police, there were no suspicious circumstances. They assume he must have collapsed taking a shortcut to his own apartment."

"Was the Kalik woman questioned at the time?"

"That, I don't know, but the Turkish police should be able to tell you."

"Was a postmortem carried out?"

"There was some sort of examination by a pathologist, but I don't think a full postmortem was carried out. The cause of death was not considered suspicious and he was buried the next day. Apparently, Simpson had 'gone native', as the Foreign and Commonwealth Office would put it. He had no family and had lost contact with the British community here.

I am told his Turkish friends arranged the funeral according to Muslim custom."

James made a mental note to find out more about Ester Kalik and his Turkish friends.

"Do you know anything about Simpson's obsession with the Cambridge Five and his theory that there had been a sixth man operating out of Istanbul?"

Tim Smith laughed.

"The old hands at the Consulate tell me that not only was he obsessed with his theory, but that he believed he had identified the sixth man—poor old Harry Haversham-Hopkiss. Harry came here in 1979, just as the Anthony Blunt scandal broke. Harry knew Blunt, might even have been a friend at one time, but I very much doubt that he ever possessed the skills or temperament for espionage. He calls himself an art connoisseur, but he was never in the same league as Blunt. He wrote a book about the early 20th-century Turkish artist Osman Hamdi Bey and paid for it to be published. I doubt if he sold a single copy, but anyone he met was liable to be presented with the book. I believe we have one somewhere in the Consulate, if you are interested. All that said, I think Simpson gave Harry a very hard time in the mid-90s as he dug around for evidence of a connection with the Cambridge spies.

"I hope you don't mind, but I have invited Andrew MacPherson to join us for dinner. Andy worked at the Consulate as a locally engaged officer for more than thirty years before retiring a few months ago. He knows more about where the skeletons in Istanbul lie than I will ever do. More to the point, he knows Harry Hopkiss well and knew Bill Simpson too."

Andrew Macpherson had arrived in Istanbul as a PhD student in 1965, met and married a local girl and had lived in Istanbul ever since. He was short, sturdily built with a shock of white hair, hints of its original red still visible. He greeted James and his former boss with a warm smile and firm handshake. Dinner passed in a stream of lively conversation, anecdotes about life in Istanbul and the changes Andy had seen over almost 60 years in the city. Andy was an excellent raconteur and, without betraying confidences, had his dinner companions in stitches with his tales of mayhem and calamity in the consular section over the years. As coffee was served, he became serious.

"You want to know about Bill Simpson and Harry Haversham-Hopkiss, I believe."

James nodded assent.

"Bill was an obsessive. It was hard to like the man, though I understand his resentment at being 'put out to grass', as he would have called it in 1993. It was less easy to understand his fixation that there had been a sixth Cambridge spy operating in Istanbul in the late 70s and 80s, and his conviction that old Harry Hopkiss was that man would have been funny if it had not been so serious; not to mention upsetting for Harry when he eventually found out what Simpson was up to."

"Could there have been anything in it?" James asked.

"I very much doubt it—though discovering that 'the nice man or woman' living quietly next door is a spy is not unknown. That said, in Harry's case, I would be more than surprised to learn that he had been a Russian agent, or anyone else's agent for that matter."

"What can you tell me about him?"

"Harry Haversham-Hopkiss—where to begin? I'm not even sure if that is the name you might find on his birth certificate. There are certainly enough stories about Harry to fill the pages of several Agatha Christie novels. When he arrived in Istanbul in 1979, he lived in the fast lane. He rented a villa on the Bosphorus and held lavish parties, inviting everyone who was anyone in town—politicians, diplomats, members of old aristocratic families, stars of stage and screen—you name it. He never married and if there was a beautiful Turkish man at his side, it was seldom the same man from one party to the next. In the traditional society in which he found himself, nothing was ever said overtly about his sexuality. On the other hand, much was said of his assumed inherited wealth. The only thing he ever did, which remotely resembled work, was to write a book about Osman Hamdi Bey—a book which did scant justice to his gifted subject.

"He may have known Kim Philby—they were both alumni of Trinity College, Cambridge, but there is nothing to suggest they were friends—Harry was twenty years younger than Philby and would have been a boy of ten when Philby was in Istanbul betraying the double agent, Konstantin Volkov. So, it's difficult to work out why Simpson thought there was a link. Anyway, Harry's flamboyant lifestyle came to an abrupt halt in 1990. The rumour was that he had spent rather than invested his inheritance. He preferred to say that his investments had 'gone south' in some unnamed financial crash. No longer the grand villa on the Bosphorus but a tiny apartment in Fener; no lavish parties unless he was invited to one by an old friend; and no beautiful young men.

"He was never on our guest list for official events like the Queen's birthday party—just the faint hint that he might have dabbled in espionage was enough to ensure that he was excluded, but he sometimes managed to appear on the arm of an elderly dowager who did have an invitation.

"Whatever the truth of the matter, Harry is now eighty-five, in poor health, alone and living on the charity of others. He is a complex character and may well have a past that doesn't bear scrutiny, but a spy? I doubt it. I could arrange for you to meet Harry, if you wish. If you say you are investigating Simpson's death, he'll probably tell you he would like to shake the hand of whoever killed him—if indeed he was killed."

In the taxi going back to his apartment, James reflected on the pleasant evening in good company. It lifted his spirits and showed Istanbul in an altogether more positive light than his first impression. He looked forward to meeting the legendary Harry Haversham-Hopkiss, whoever he was. Sleep eluded him that night. Something kept nagging at the back of his mind—something to do with the date at which Harry's fortunes had abruptly changed—1990. Not long after President Gorbachev had introduced glasnost, making fundamental changes to the political structure in Russia and instigating a rapprochement with the west. One year after the Berlin Wall came down—redundancy notices for many former spies would have followed. Could Harry's sudden change in circumstances have been linked?

*

Harry answered the phone on the second ring—indicating that he was either lonely and hopeful of some companionship, or waiting for an important call.

"Hello Mr Haversham-Hopkiss, I am James Davidson. A mutual friend of ours, Andy Macpherson, suggested contacting you as I am new to Istanbul, and he tells me that you know more than anyone about life in this city."

"Please call me Harry—everyone does. Yes, Andy told me you might get in touch, and I would be delighted to meet you. I don't see as many people as I used to these days so name your time and place and I'll be there."

"May I offer you lunch tomorrow at Sarnic? Do you know the restaurant?"

"Splendid, my dear boy, just splendid. It used to be one of my favourite haunts when I had money to throw around. Shall we say 1 pm?"

James put the phone down with a smile. Was Harry genuinely an old duffer from a bygone era, or was he a consummate actor? The next day would tell.

Chapter 2
At Sarnic Restaurant

James did not need to be an MI6 officer to identify Harry immediately. Harry sat at a corner table brandishing a closely studied menu while chatting animatedly to a patient waiter. James smiled as he heard the undeniable, English upper-class bark carrying through into Harry's fluent Turkish. In the moments before Harry spotted him, James took in the sparse grey hair combed carefully above a round, florid face, the prominent nose and searching eyes. As he neared the table, he could see faint scar tissue along Harry's upper lip and jaw line—more obvious now on ageing skin than it would have been in his youth. Harry was resplendent in a checked shirt and red waistcoat, both in danger of losing the battle to contain the underlying girth. However reduced his circumstances, Harry was clearly not starving.

Harry paused and stood up as he saw James approaching.

"My dear boy, I am delighted to make your acquaintance. Do sit down." Struggling to extricate his hand from the vigorous handshake, James couldn't help feeling that he was cast in the role of guest—a role he would be required to relinquish as soon as the bill appeared.

"Before we get down to the serious business of the day, shall we order?" Harry's question had all the subtlety of a command. "As you are new to Istanbul, allow me to order for you." James sat back, both amused and mildly irritated, but secretly relieved that he did not have to engage with an unfamiliar menu in a language he struggled to read. He also guessed that he would get no information from Harry until food was on its way.

"What brings you to Istanbul at this dismal time of year, James?—You don't mind if I call you James, do you?"

Anything was better than being called 'dear boy'! "Of course not. I have taken early retirement and have found it rather hard to adjust to having time on my hands, so decided to travel. I must confess, I hadn't realised that winter in Istanbul would be quite so cold, otherwise I might have started off elsewhere. However, now that I am here, I would like to get to know the city."

"What did you do before retiring, if I may ask?"

"I was a civil servant."

"Aha! I had you down as a policeman!"

Perhaps Harry was not quite the old buffoon he pretended to be.

"What made you think I was a policeman?"

"Oh, a lifetime of people-watching in a city with more than its fair share of policemen, intelligence agents and spies mingling among the tourists and locals. Just something about your demeanour."

James gave a brief laugh which even to his own ears sounded false. To his great relief, the food arrived, drawing Harry's attention away from establishing James's occupational credentials.

The meal was delicious. Harry had ordered a vast vegetable mezze, followed by spinach tart and skewers of delicately spiced lamb. An impressive array of awards adorned the label on the bottle of rosé which arrived with the food—presumably the basis of its eye-watering price. James couldn't help smiling as he imagined the reaction of the bean-counters in London when they received his expenses claim. A tray of delicate little pastries—demolished by Harry at lightning speed—and Turkish coffee concluded the meal. Replete, Harry turned his mind to the task of introducing his companion to the delights and quirks of the city he called home.

He seemed to have forgotten about establishing who James was and why he was in Istanbul, or had he just decided to let it go for the moment? Either way, James was pleased that the conversation could move on. There was more to Harry than appeared at first glance and more than once James was aware of a fleeting, calculating look in the cold, blue eyes.

Harry did have a wealth of diverting stories to tell about the rich and famous in Istanbul, tales of shady characters and outright villains, and surprisingly sensitive reflections on daily life for the ordinary citizens of the city. He made little reference to the political situation and advised James to avoid talking about it to anyone he didn't know well. Harry visibly relaxed as the best part of the bottle of wine—James had limited himself to one glass—took effect. The slight tension of the first moments had disappeared, so much so that James risked asking, "Did you ever meet a chap called Bill Simpson here?"

He watched as all vestiges of relaxed bonhomie vanished. Harry's response was terse, "What is your interest in Bill Simpson?"

"Nothing, really. He was at school with an old friend of mine, and we heard he had died very suddenly."

"You seem to have a lot of old friends, James. First Andy Macpherson, and now a friend who knew Bill Simpson." Harry's tone was ice-cold.

"I guess I do—have a lot of friends, I mean. It was just that Simpson had been in good health as far as we knew, so his death came as a bit of a surprise."

"Simpson was in anything but good health; he was seventy-five and a drunk. His death surprised no one here."

"I take it you didn't like him very much."

"Like him! The man was deranged, obsessed with spy-catching, although there were no spies to catch, and no one who would have been interested even if he claimed to have found one."

James was aware of the exchange becoming very heated. "Did he think he had identified a spy?"

"Of course, he hadn't. The man was mad—simultaneously sleeping with a girl from the Russian Consulate and with Ester Kalik of all people! Pillow-talk with the GRU (Russian Intelligence) and MIT (Turkish Intelligence). If, as you seem to be hinting, his death was suspicious, choose your assassin! I wouldn't get on the wrong side of Kalik if I could avoid it—Bill was actively courting disaster. She would kill for stealing her sandwich, let alone for stealing her man. I don't know anything about the Russian girl."

Something about the way he dismissed the Russian—not least referring to her as a 'girl'—did not ring true. Harry got to his feet, the bonhomie once more in evidence.

"How time flies in good company. Thank you for a delightful lunch, James, and for our very interesting conversation. I am sure we shall meet again, and I am glad my intuition is as sharp as ever. I had you down as a policeman—or something of that order." With a conspiratorial smile, he left the table with remarkable alacrity for so large a man, expertly avoiding the waiter approaching with the bill.

Whatever Harry was, he was not just an old buffoon.

With the card-melting bill settled, James headed back to his apartment. What had Bill Simpson been up to? Hats off to a seventy-five-year-old man who kept two women happy in bed despite twin handicaps of age and alcohol addiction! Or was sex not what these relationships were about? Secondly, why would younger, possibly much younger, women want to be in a relationship with a septuagenarian Englishman with a drink problem? As far as James could work out, neither woman needed rescuing from spinsterhood, or from a life of poverty or vice. There was no indication that Bill Simpson had possessed the kind of conspicuous wealth that might have compensated for any shortcomings as a lover.

The name, Ester Kalik, had come up in conversation twice now—first in London then at the Consulate General the night before. She was apparently a senior officer with MIT. What had she really wanted out of her relationship with Simpson? Was Simpson on a watch list with Turkish Intelligence, and if so, why? James could think of no reason. It was perhaps easier to guess what the woman employed at the Russian Consulate might have wanted out of tedious nights with an old

Englishman. James laughed at himself—was he just jealous? He was a fit, reasonably attractive (so he had been told by several match-making friends) divorced man, more than twenty years younger than Simpson, but without one—let alone two—women in his bed.

Chapter 3
Istanbul

"It's Harry, Ester. Apologies for calling at so late an hour, but I couldn't get hold of you earlier. Is it ok to talk right now?"

"Yes. What time is it? I must have dozed off."

"Midnight—sorry, but a curious thing happened today. At the suggestion of a contact at the British Consulate, I had lunch with an Englishman, James Davidson. Name mean anything to you?"

"No. Who is he?"

"Says he is a newly retired British civil servant, travelling to fill in the hours of unaccustomed freedom. Thing is, he has MI5 or MI6 written all over him."

"Istanbul in January is certainly a strange place to start a geriatric gap year."

"Stranger still is his interest in the fate of our erstwhile acquaintance, Mr Simpson!"

"You're kidding!"

"Unfortunately not. We need to talk…"

*

Harry poured himself a generous measure of whisky and put on a recording of Rosalynd Tureck playing Bach's *Goldberg Variations* to calm his nerves. His unlikely friendship with Ester went back a long way, to a rail journey from Istanbul to Ankara. They were alone in a first-class carriage at the rear of the train when the PKK set off a bomb which derailed the engine and the first three carriages.

They were in the middle of nowhere, snow was falling and the lights and heating in their carriage had gone out. Daylight was fading as he opened the carriage door to see what had happened, closing it almost immediately as a gust of freezing snow blew in. Returning to his compartment, he noticed his fellow passenger huddled on the floor, shaking uncontrollably. He crouched down beside her, doing his best to sound reassuring and helped her back onto her seat, but the shivering just got worse.

"Sorry," she had said. "I was caught in an explosion which killed my mother and brother when I was seven. The noise—it all just came back to me. Sorry, sorry …"

"No need to be sorry," he had replied. "This is scary for everyone, and goodness knows how long we will have to wait for help to arrive, so we will just have to make the best of it. Let me introduce myself, I am Harry Hopkiss."

Ester had stared at him for a moment before asking, "Where are you from?"

"That's a very good question," Harry had replied. "I have an expired UK passport that says I am British. My current identity card states that I am now a Turkish citizen, but it is likely that neither of these attributions is the truth, the whole truth and nothing but the truth."

"What on earth do you mean?" Ester had asked, wondering whether this strange man was a singularly indiscreet foreign agent, or simply delusional.

Afterwards, Harry never knew what had prompted him to tell Ester his story, other than that it had provided a distraction for both.

At the end of the Second World War, Harry had been found by a British doctor in a refugee camp run by the Red Cross just south of Berlin. He was about one year old, nameless and severely disfigured. The doctor in question, Randolph Haversham-Hopkiss, was a plastic surgeon and saw in Harry the perfect subject on which to practice his art and establish his name. He adopted Harry and took him back to London.

Harry spent much of the following five years in and out of hospital as the eminent surgeon documented his progress in transforming Harry's facial deformity into the unmarked face of a normal six-year-old boy. This notable success was widely reported in the Lancet and in national newspapers. To his adoptive father, Harry was a patient, not a son. His wife made no secret of the fact that she did not want the boy in either capacity. A nanny, Lucy, had provided all the mothering Harry had ever known until he was packed off to boarding school at the age of eight. To his utter dismay, when he came home for his first Christmas break, Lucy had gone—'ran off to get married without leaving an address', according to his parents. Even at eight, Harry had known better—no point spending money on a nanny when the boy was away at school for much of the year.

Unfortunately, the publicity surrounding Harry's surgery meant that several of the boys at school knew the story, and one child had embellished the tale by asserting that skin from his backside had been grafted onto his face, earning Harry the nickname, 'Arseface'. The nickname stuck until the day when, aged ten, Harry realised that he was taller and stronger than his tormentors and beat two of them up in the dormitory one night, to loud cheers from their dorm-mates. The noise woke the housemaster, and Harry endured the inevitable reprisals from the housemaster and his father with gritted teeth—but the name-calling stopped.

That was until two years later, when one of his earlier tormentors told everyone that Harry had been found by the Red Cross in Germany, so his real father must have been a Nazi. It was not until he went up to Cambridge in 1962 that he finally escaped from tales of his strange adoption, his miraculous surgery and the home where he was of no further use, neither wanted nor needed.

By the time Harry fell silent, Ester had recovered—the violent shaking reduced to a faint tremor which had more to do with the rapidly falling temperature than with fear. She felt she owed it to him to relate a little of her own story. She had been born Ester Arafat in Gaza. Her family was not related to Yasser Arafat, the Palestinian leader who held the western world to account for many years for its failure to recognise the Palestinian state, but they were proud to share his name. She lived with her mother and older brother in a one-room flat in Gaza city—her father having died in an Israeli prison before she was born.

On her seventh birthday, she had gone to the market with her mother and brother to buy some special treats, an expedition that turned into a nightmare and changed her life forever. She was badly injured in a car bomb blast that killed her mother and brother, along with scores of other shoppers and stall-holders. Popular rhetoric at the time blamed the Israelis, but on much later reflection, she accepted that suicide bombing was not the way Israelis did things. This was more likely to have been a bomb that had gone off prematurely as the car was being driven towards an Israeli or American target.

Ester was taken to a field hospital run by the Red Crescent and, when no relatives appeared to claim her, a Turkish nurse decided to adopt her and take her back to Istanbul. Unlike Harry's experience, she had been well cared for in her new home, but her abiding hatred of Israelis and Americans deepened as she grew older and would define the rest of her life. Kalik, the name by which she had long been known, was her adoptive mother's name. Arafat was not a safe surname to have beyond the confines of Gaza.

An unlikely friendship was born that day. Two people drawn together by childhood trauma and unresolved questions about identity and nationhood.

*

Harry was never sure why he had been seduced by the offer of Russian 'gold' in his final year at Cambridge. The approach had been skilful, making light of the substance of the proposal. His contact knew that Harry had been offered a job with an internationally renowned investment bank in the city, one with links to government departments and other national institutions. Harry felt no particular loyalty to England—a country that had provided expert medical treatment and a good education, but little else. He had always felt an outsider, at home, at school, and even at Cambridge. He knew he was probably ethnically German, or perhaps Jewish. He hadn't been circumcised, but there would have been no facilities for circumcision at the camps by the time he was born, and he was in all likelihood a child of the camps—or just possibly an orphan of Allied bombing, or a foundling. He would never know.

Three years after leaving Cambridge, Harry was making a name for himself in the cut and thrust of the financial world. Work absorbed his waking hours, and he had almost forgotten about the Russian proposal when, to his surprise, his contact called him. In exchange for valuable snippets of financial information, Harry's personal wealth increased steadily, and he used his expertise to place his Russian 'fees' in a range of accounts and investments that were unlikely to come to the attention of Her Majesty's Revenue and Customs.

That was until he made a mistake, creating a potential financial scandal that could have rocked the very foundations of the prestigious institution which paid his legitimate salary and bonuses. An internal audit had uncovered his dealings with Oleg Peskov, a cultural attaché at the Russian Embassy. The chief executive of the bank, the MI5 Director General and a senior government minister held a damage limitation meeting at an exclusive club in St James. At the meeting, they agreed that the 'irregularities' uncovered were retrievable; that they did not constitute a risk to national security, in particular to financial security; furthermore, that going public with the findings would result in serious reputational damage to the bank, embarrassment to the government, and risk halting the gradual warming of relationships with Russia.

The decision was a gagging order and exile for Harry if he wished to remain at liberty; and an immediate requirement for Peskov to pursue his diplomatic career elsewhere. Harry had no hesitation in opting for exile, eventually ending up in Istanbul.

Bill Simpson had been an MI6 operative at the time and word had drifted across the river of a cover-up involving an investment bank, MI5 and a Russian diplomat. He was convinced that the sudden disappearance of a rising star at the bank was linked to the cover-up, but try as he might, he had been unable to break through the wall of silence surrounding the rumoured affair. His obsession with identifying a 'sixth man' spying for the Russians stemmed from this time, and he would spend years trying to trace the missing banker, finally tracking him down in Istanbul.

Chapter 4
An Apartment in Fatih, Istanbul

Ester stared at Harry in silence—an unnerving silence, dark eyes betraying no trace of emotion. Harry shuffled nervously on the edge of his seat, desperate for a drink he knew would not be offered.

"So, what exactly was your lunchtime companion's interest in Bill Simpson?"

"I couldn't work it out. He said Simpson was an old friend with whom he had lost contact and had been concerned to hear of his sudden death. While he was in Istanbul, he thought he should try to find out what had happened to him as the information received by his family had been sketchy. A barely believable cover story for an MI5 or MI6 agent, which I believe him to be."

"I didn't think Simpson had any family!"

"Neither did I, but apparently there is a sister living in Bedfordshire."

"And you said the only reason James Davidson wanted to meet you was because someone at the Consulate said you might know something about Simpson?"

"Yes, old Andy Macpherson apparently told him that I was better informed than the CIA on the lives, liaisons, and deaths of expats in Istanbul!"

"Are you sure that was the only reason for wanting to meet you? If Davidson is an MI5/MI6 officer, he presumably knows about your involvement in the Peskov affair—and may also know that Peskov's son Igor was, until very recently, attached to the Russian Embassy in Ankara."

"I can't think why Davidson would be interested in me. I have posed no threat to British security for decades, and my only contact with Igor Peskov recently was when I introduced him to you. He did contact me early on, but when I explained that I no longer had any inside information on financial dealings in the city of London, he lost interest. What your interest in Peskov junior was, is no concern of mine. Let's just hope the mysterious circumstances surrounding the deaths of Peskov and Simpson remain mysterious."

Ester remained silent. She regretted having had to kill Igor Peskov. The only killing she had ever regretted. He was the only lover who had ever satisfied her sexually—he liked it rough and in his bed she had discovered she liked it rough too. For three years, their mutual interest in sex and in what the CIA and Mossad were up to in Istanbul coincided, and they had occasionally shared intelligence. Caught up in the sexual thrill of their relationship, she had uncharacteristically lowered her guard, only to learn that Igor had been less romantically distracted than she was.

During months of covert surveillance, he had amassed evidence of her secret affiliation to a militant Palestinian organisation. His attempt to use that information to induce her to pass on details of MIT activity around the Black Sea coast would prove to be a serious miscalculation, one which would cost him his life. Ester disliked betrayal. His alcohol- and drug-saturated body was found on derelict ground by workmen taking a shortcut to a nearby building site. They did not notice the puncture mark on his arm, but the pathologist did ...and was shortly afterwards persuaded not to notice it.

After Igor's death, she had spent several anxious months worrying that he might have left a file on her links with the Palestinian organisation in the Russian Embassy in Ankara or at the Russian Consulate General in Istanbul. She feared the telephone call that would threaten to expose her involvement with the Palestinians, unless she agreed to pass on classified information. That phone call never came, and she had just begun to relax when Bill Simpson entered her life. Continuing his obsessive pursuit of the sixth man, Bill was on the Peskov trail, hoping it would lead him to his prey.

It was Harry who alerted her to Simpson's relationship with a new cultural attaché at the Russian Consulate. What possible reason could an attractive young woman have for getting involved with a physical and psychological wreck like Simpson? There was only one distinctly disquieting possibility—that the Russians did have evidence of her dealings with the Palestinians and were biding their time before deciding how to best to use this information. The attaché's presumed assignment—to find out if there was more to learn from Bill during pillow-talk.

Ester had endured Simpson's drunken fumbling until she was convinced that he knew nothing of Igor Peskov's research into her background. A conviction she would live to regret. If he knew nothing, there was nothing he could pass on to the Turkish authorities—or so she had believed. However, one night, she had found him rifling through papers he had managed to extract from the locked drawers of her desk. He had become a dangerous liability. Disposing of Simpson had not caused her a moment's regret. The Turkish police would waste little time investigating the death of an elderly, overweight Englishman with diabetes and advanced cirrhosis of the liver.

In this, she was correct but had a few sleepless nights when she heard that Commander Kadir Demercol of the Istanbul Directorate of Police had asked to see the autopsy report. If there was one policeman that she admired and feared in equal measure, it was Kadir Demercol, and Demercol had never made any secret of his exasperation at the reluctance of MIT to share intelligence. She knew Demercol had worked with the British police on two high-profile cases, so perhaps he was just checking that nothing had been overlooked in investigating and recording the death of a former British intelligence officer—nothing that could cause future embarrassment.

However, worries about what the Russians might know persisted. And now another—allegedly ex—British intelligence officer, James Davidson, was poking his nose into Simpson's death. She needed to talk to Davidson and deal with him if he posed a threat. The strain was beginning to tell.

*

James had been pondering how best to contact Ester Kalik. In his current ambiguous position, a direct agency-to-agency request would raise too many questions. Then there was the uncertainty over the nature of her relationship with

Simpson. If it had been an entirely private affair, she might not take kindly to intrusive questioning. If there had been some clandestine motivation, she would take even less kindly to interference. None of the adjectives used to describe this woman who had defied gender norms to reach the top of MIT tempted him to make a false move. Thus, it was both a surprise and a relief when Harry called to say that Kalik wanted to meet him.

The following afternoon, as instructed, James approached a park bench outside the Malta Pavilion in Yildiz Park. Wisps of freezing mist drifted on an icy wind coming straight from the Bosphorus. As he neared the Malta Pavilion, James could make out a lone figure apparently studying the neo-classical frontage of the building, formerly a prison for high-ranking detainees including Sultan Murad V, now housing a popular café. A tourist would have made straight for the café to escape from the penetrating cold instead of pacing back and forth in a futile attempt to keep warm. James's high hopes of respite in the café would shortly be dashed in favour of a park bench.

Ester saw him approach. Harry was right—this man had intelligence service written all over him. What Harry had not mentioned, surprisingly given his orientation, was that the man was extraordinarily handsome. He was tall, clean-shaven, and his neatly cut fair hair, greying slightly at the temples, framed matinée-idol features. Costly winter weather clothing hinted at an underlying athletic build. An irreverent thought flashed through her mind—if she had to use sex to get this man to divulge his purposes, it would be no hardship. Perhaps he was too much the English gentleman to put sex on a war-footing the way Igor had done—though you never could tell, but an infinitely more enticing prospect than the stomach-churning sessions she had endured with Bill Simpson.

She took in the cool, appraising look as he sat alongside her on a park bench. This man was in a different league from Bill Simpson. She was immediately on her guard but couldn't help responding to his disarming smile. James noticed that her smile did not touch her dark eyes. What lay behind the blank gaze—suspicion, hatred, fear—some dark chasm? He didn't know what he had expected, but not this slight woman in her late forties, attractive in a forbidding sort of way, her raven hair loosely held in a Ferragamo scarf.

"I'll come straight to the point," Ester said without preamble. "I believe you are seeking information about Bill Simpson, and it would be interesting to know why."

"The direct approach is often best," James said with another flash of the beguiling smile, "especially in sub-zero temperatures when the notion of lingering is not altogether appealing. So, why my interest in Bill Simpson? When I entered government service many years ago, Bill Simpson and a woman called Eileen Harriman were rising stars, working together on a special project. To everyone's surprise, they both took early retirement and went their separate ways—he to Istanbul and she to Sydney.

"The odd coincidence—if it is a coincidence—is that they both died within days of each other on opposite sides of the world. In our line of work, we instinctively distrust coincidences; wouldn't you agree? We know Simpson continued to obsess about a British national living in Istanbul and spying for the Russians. To use your own expression, we would find it interesting to know whether this was fantasy or reality. If the latter, we would like to know what, if anything, he had uncovered. We know you were on friendly terms and wonder if you can shed any light on the matter."

Ester remained silent—and expressionless if you discounted the cold penetrating stare. James did not discount it and wondered if he had overplayed his hand. Finally, she spoke, "We were not friends, we were acquainted. We knew of Simpson's obsessive search for a British spy, but we had to ask ourselves what a former financier and unsuccessful art historian who had lived in Istanbul for almost forty years—yes, we know who Simpson had set his sights on—could know that might interest the Russians.

"Harry Haversham-Hopkiss did not travel to UK; he did not receive visitors from the UK; he was not on the British Embassy or Consulate guest list; he had no access to military contacts or bases. Harry Hopkiss was never charged with spying. As far as we know, Harry has posed no risk to UK security since his arrival in Istanbul. Anything he may have done in the distant past is of no present consequence. The geopolitical situation has changed out of all recognition since the time Harry and Oleg Peskov were chums."

If James was surprised by how much Ester knew, he didn't show it.

"So, why MIT's recent interest in Bill Simpson if you believed he was chasing a chimera? Why suddenly after so many years? I can only assume that MIT interests lay behind your sudden 'friendship' with Bill Simpson. It could hardly have been for reasons of personal pleasure."

Did he catch a flicker of annoyance or anger in Ester's otherwise blank gaze? After a while, she spoke, measuring her words carefully. "We wanted to ensure that nothing Simpson was doing posed a risk to Turkish security."

It was James's turn to remain silent. Ester's hint of a risk to Turkish security made no sense whatsoever. Simpson passing Turkish secrets to a hostile state—via his Russian girlfriend? It was laughable. The man would have had no access to anything that the Turkish authorities wished to keep secret. He decided to let the matter drop for the time being. As he looked up, he was aware of Ester scrutinising his face.

"Ester, if we stay here much longer, we may turn into blocks of ice. It has been good to meet you—perhaps we might meet in more convivial circumstances before I leave. Over dinner perhaps."

Ester was on the point of refusing when he added, "I am dining with Kadir and Ayşe Demercol tomorrow evening, but perhaps the evening after if you are free."

If he was dining with Demercol, she had to know what that was about. She would accept his invitation, besides … he was undeniably attractive. She would need to be on her guard though. This man was astute, and he hadn't believed the reason she had given for MIT interest in Bill Simpson. He must not discover that it was she, not MIT, who had to know if Simpson had learned anything of interest from his Russian 'contact'—anything that could result in a charge of treason for the first woman to get near the top of MIT.

Chapter 5
Villa Demercaol

James had felt slightly diffident about phoning Commander Demercol to suggest a meeting to discuss nothing more serious than the death of an elderly English expat in apparently unsuspicious circumstances. He knew the commander would have much more important tasks on his desk. To his surprise, the switchboard at police headquarters put him through at once and the voice on the other end of the line greeted him pleasantly, and in excellent English—to his intense relief. He explained the purpose of his call and, to his surprise, Demercol simply said, "I apologise, I am rather tight for time at the moment. Why don't you come for dinner this evening? If you arrive around seven, we can talk in private first. My wife has invited two young Argentinians to stay with us for a day or two, so conversation at dinner will need to be general. I can arrange for a cab to pick you up if you let me have your address."

"That's very kind, and I appreciate being given the opportunity to talk with you in private. However, if you have house guests, I should not intrude on dinner arrangements."

"Actually, it will ease matters if you stay for dinner, if that is all right with you."

"In that case, I will be delighted to join you," James replied, hoping there was no trace of puzzlement in the tone of his voice. It was odd to say, 'My wife has invited', rather than, 'We have invited'; and what did he mean when he said his presence would 'ease matters'? Maybe the young Argentinians were rowdy, ungracious teenagers belonging to a friend of his wife's.

*

James began to relax and enjoy the scenery as his cab left the bustling city centre to drive along the southern banks of the Bosphorus, passing ever more opulent villas with beautifully kept gardens sweeping down to the shoreline. When the cab finally turned off the main highway and began its ascent up the driveway to a stunningly beautiful historic Turkish mansion, he allowed himself a pang of pure envy. He had been told that Kadir Demercol belonged to a distinguished aristocratic family who could trace their ancestry back to the Byzantine era, but nothing had prepared him for the beauty of this place, and he envied the young Argentinians their opportunity to spend some time there—he hoped they appreciated it. He was met at the door by a beautiful woman, possibly in her late fifties but with that timeless grace and charm that renders age irrelevant.

"You are very welcome, Mr Davidson. I hope the journey out here wasn't too tiresome."

"Not at all," James replied as he shook the proffered hand, glad that she had initiated the gesture as he was not quite sure of the etiquette of greeting a Turkish woman. "As soon as the cab set off, I switched to tourist mode and enjoyed the journey."

"Please come in. My husband is on a call but will be with you shortly. Let me show you to the library and I shall arrange for some tea to be brought." James thought of his post-divorce flat in central London and thought how nice it would be to live in a place like this, with a beautiful woman to welcome him home with offers of tea. Wine would be better, but tea would be fine. Oh, the sin of envy!

As he followed Ayşe Demercol across the spacious hall, a slim man in his early thirties slowed his descent down the magnificent, curved staircase. He was dressed in a black sweater and black jeans—something about him reminded James of a priest.

"Good evening, Mrs Demercol, Sir. I apologise for intruding; I was just going out for a stroll in the garden. Please excuse me."

"Of course, Federico. You are not disturbing us at all but keep to the lit paths—it is rather cold and dark out there. Federico is one of the two Argentinians staying with us just now. You will meet them both at dinner."

So, not ungracious, rowdy teenagers then, James thought. But Federico was clearly not at ease, whatever the reason.

Demercol was waiting in the library as James entered.

"Welcome. I'm Kadir Demercol. Please make yourself at home."

"James Davidson. Thank you very much for seeing me."

"It's a pleasure—now, what can I do for you?"

"As you know, my fellow countryman, Bill Simpson, has been a thorn in the flesh for many people in Istanbul over the last twenty years—throwing barely credible allegations around, making enemies—and some rather surprising friends, Ester Kalik and an attaché at the Russian Consulate to name but two. I am on a semi-official quest to establish exactly what he was up to and whether there were any suspicious circumstances surrounding his death. I realise that the death of a tiresome British expat will not have been at the top of your in-tray, but I wondered if you or any of your colleagues might be able to shed any light on this."

Kadir was sitting opposite James, hands steepled against his face, seemingly deep in thought.

"I called up Mr Simpson's pathology report."

"Oh." James failed to keep the surprise out of his voice.

"Yes. I asked for it because the last person to see him alive was Ester Kalik, and that alone is enough to make me suspicious. Not surprisingly, she has covered herself with a cast-iron alibi, but given who she is, I would expect nothing less. In the last few months of his life, Mr Simpson was seeing a lot of her, but I have been unable to establish why. I can't believe it was personal. Mr Simpson was much older, in very poor shape and Kalik doesn't do personal relationships.

"The path report stated that he died of cardiac arrest—as we all do—brought on by consumption of alcohol and cocaine. The levels of both found in his system were not necessarily fatal, although given his poor state of health, they might just have triggered a heart attack. That said, several things trouble me about the cause of death. It was two days before Simpson's body was found on waste-ground, and a further two days at the morgue before anyone got around to examining his body or carrying out tests.

"His death and its reported causes bear a remarkable similarity to an earlier murder, that of Igor Peskov—friend and almost certainly lover of Ester Kalik. More suspicious yet, part of the path report has been redacted—skilfully, but not so skilfully that we didn't notice. The pathologist told us he had been so tired he had mistakenly entered findings from another case, hence the deletion. He is a very poor liar."

"What do you make of Ester Kalik?"

"Who was it who was described as mad, bad and dangerous to know?"

"Lord Byron, according to Caroline Lamb."

"Well, Kalik isn't mad, but the other two adjectives apply. She is cold, calculating and very clever. However, with two unexplained and rather messy deaths so close to her door, I am beginning to wonder if she is losing her edge. Either that, or she has a secret that Peskov and Simpson may have threatened to disclose—a secret best kept from MIT, perhaps. On the other hand, the similarities in the two cases may just be coincidental…"

"It sounds as if you suspect that she was involved in both deaths. What kind of a hold could either man have had on Kalik?"

"Kalik wasn't born in Türkiye although she is a Turkish citizen. She was born in Palestine and lost her family at the age of seven when a car bomb went off in a crowded marketplace. She was eventually adopted by a Turkish nurse and brought to Istanbul, but I have often wondered where her true loyalties lie. As a leading Jesuit[4] famously said, 'Give me a child till he is seven and he is mine for life.' I have not a shred of evidence to substantiate doubts about her loyalty, but

---

[4] *Ignatius Loyola: 1491-1556: Founder of the Society of Jesus—the Jesuits.*

there is something strange about her total lack of emotional engagement with this country and its people, though no one could fault her diligence on behalf of Türkiye's security service. She is an enigma."

"This is all rather disquieting. I have invited her to dinner tomorrow evening!"

"Sit with your back to the wall, order your own transport and don't eat, smoke or drink anything she offers you," Kadir said, a rare smile lightening the mood.

"Thank you, this has been very helpful," James replied, "though I am left with more questions than answers."

"We'll be called to dinner soon and before we go, I should just say something about our other guests. They are from Buenos Aires. Father Federico Alvarez is a Jesuit priest and delightful company. However, I find myself in difficulty relating to his friend, Dr Jens Timmerman. It is not Jens's fault, and I am sure he finds the whole situation as awkward as I do. You see, he has only recently found out that Jan-Marten Timmerman, the man he always thought was his father, is not his biological father.

"This would be a difficult revelation for anyone, but what he has found out is beyond horrific. Jens's biological father was Hans Peter von Seidel, a man I arrested on one count of conspiracy to murder, two counts of actual murder, one count of attempted murder, and possession of a vast horde of stolen art held in a vault in Istanbul."

"The Nazi war criminal? It was all over the news for months."

"It was. And the crimes he committed in Türkiye paled in comparison to the atrocities he carried out during World War II. There was also a murder in Edinburgh to add to his account. My difficulty with Jens is that he looks so like his biological father. Just glancing at him takes me back to the awful days, cooped up in an interview room interrogating the monster, listening to that grating, soulless voice demanding sympathy for the personal betrayals he believed had led to his capture. Not a hint of remorse in all the hours I spent feeling contaminated by his evil presence.

"I am shocked at myself for visiting the sins of the father on the son; he doesn't deserve it, and we are both struggling with the situation. Forgive me, but that is why I said your presence at dinner might ease matters. Ayşe believes that people lucky enough to live in large houses should offer hospitality to whoever needs it. In this case, she suggested the two men stay here without thinking of the implications. She also thinks I need to grow up and get over it! But she was lucky enough never to have met von Seidel."

"Heavens! I thought you might have been seeking salvation from a couple of rowdy kids. Not something as dramatic as this. Like you, I have encountered some very bad people in the course of my work, and it does leave an indelible mark. But never with anyone as evil as von Seidel. What a difficult situation—I feel for you all. I'll do my best at dinner. But before we go, can you tell me why Jens and Federico are in Istanbul?"

"Apparently, against everyone's advice, Jens decided to trace his father's footsteps across Europe to Istanbul, to the courtroom where he was tried and the prison where he died. Morbid, but understandable. I think he underestimated the emotional impact of doing this, which is why Federico has come out to join him for part of the journey."

As James was led into the dining room by Ayşe, he couldn't help thinking that this assignment/non-assignment was turning out to be a lot more interesting, complex and downright dangerous than he could possibly have imagined. Over dinner, he admired Father Federico's skill at keeping the conversation alive with tales of the pair's travels in Europe. He immediately filled any uncomfortable silences with queries about places to visit in Istanbul and Ayşe's work at a mosque refuge centre.

Turning his attention to me, Federico was amused to learn that I had spent my schooldays at a Jesuit college in England. James envied the way in which Federico kept discussion afloat, avoiding the diplomatic rocks—a skill no doubt honed as shepherd of a large ethnically and socially diverse parish community in Buenos Aires.

*

Ester had suggested an elegant Italian restaurant in a surprisingly quiet corner of Sultanahmet. James arrived slightly early but after twenty minutes and several solicitous approaches by waiters, began to wonder if he had been stood up. He was in the process of deciding whether to dine alone or make his excuses, when she appeared, taking his breath away and that of other envious male diners. Her glossy black hair, no longer enveloped in Ferragamo silk, fell loosely in gentle waves over her shoulders. A magnificent gold torque drew all eyes to the emerald-green cocktail dress on which it lay, and to the hints of a perfect figure below.

The second thought that passed through James's mind was, *This woman could not have been the lover of a man like*

Bill Simpson—the first thought having been decidedly less professional. He stood up to welcome her as a waiter ushered her to her seat and was rewarded with the ghost of a smile. Initial bursts of conversation were stilted and kept to safe ground—the excellent choice of restaurant, the menu, the wretched weather and events on the world stage, but warmed up when they discovered a mutual love of history, which both had taken as a first degree.

Conversation moved on to the long and troubled history of the middle east and although the topic under discussion was history, both knew this was a sizing-up exercise. The tone of delivery suddenly became charged as Ester ventured into the murky waters of British and European interventions in Palestine from Balfour onwards. James maintained a respectful silence. He remembered she was Palestinian by birth and had lived there till she was seven. The surprise outburst also told him how raw the issue was for her, how very close to the otherwise impenetrable facade.

Realising that she had let her guard slip, Ester quickly returned to safer ground—"Why did you retire early from your 'government' position?" The word 'government' was said with a hint of irony.

"Well, I am recently divorced and was tired of a job that was becoming more stressful and less rewarding by the day. I felt I needed a complete change and time to recalibrate. What about you?"

"Oh, I am still working for the Ministry of the Interior. It is an important job at a time when Türkiye is surrounded by war-torn states, with lawless militant groups spilling across borders."

It was at this point that James's vague sense that she was coming on to him became more than a suspicion. He found her scarily attractive, much as an inexpert skier might feel contemplating an Olympic ski jump—the wild, unrealistic, exhilarating dream of success; the near certainty of life-changing failure. He smiled, pulling back from the brink—*What am I thinking! I'd probably end up tied to her bedposts, being horse-whipped! And found dead on waste-ground sometime later.*

She noticed the smile. "Something amusing you?"

"No, not at all. I was just thinking how much I have enjoyed this evening and I hope we can do this again soon."

"That would be good. And perhaps the next time, which I hope *will* be soon, we can get around to talking about Bill Simpson and his demons."

James's phone rang as he entered his apartment. It was Kadir Demercol.

"Just checking that you have survived the dining experience."

James laughed. He liked this man. "It all went well, though we kept on safe ground. No mention of Bill Simpson or Harry Haversham-Hopkiss. That is being reserved for round two!"

"Just tread carefully. Kalik is dangerous on all sorts of levels. Don't hesitate to call me if you need to."

Kadir was aware of Kalik's medusa-like skill as a seductress. He was also sure that Kalik was behind the deaths of Igor Peskov and Bill Simpson. He did not know why, and he had no proof, but he knew she was responsible. For that reason, Chief Inspector Djavid and his wife had dined at the same restaurant that night, tasked with ensuring James's safety.

Kadir was relieved to discover that he had underestimated James's ability to resist temptation.

Chapter 6
Argentina 2010

Jens Timmerman had spent a very happy childhood in Buenos Aires. The adored son of Maria-Silvia Martinez and Jan-Marten Timmerman, he had sailed effortlessly through school combining just enough study-time to ensure good exam results with his passion for football, horse-riding and good times with a wide circle of friends. His parents came from very different strands of Argentinian society. His maternal grandfather was a retired general who had worked closely with a succession of right-wing regimes. Jens found him decidedly scary but loved his timid grandmother who had never forgiven her husband for throwing Maria-Silvia out of the family home at the age of sixteen, leaving her prey to a predator who had held her a virtual captive for four years.

His father came from a family of human rights lawyers of Dutch descent. When his grandfather Timmerman retired, he and his wife had moved to a large house in the country, where Jens had spent the carefree summers of his childhood. The only shadow on his happiness was the increasing frailty of his little sister, Grazia. He was in his final year as a medical student when her kidneys finally failed, and the search was on for a donor. Jens volunteered without a second thought and was taken aback by his mother's reaction.

"You can't afford to be ill just before your finals. Donating a kidney is not a simple matter. We will find someone else." Jens had stared at his mother in utter incomprehension. He was surely the best chance of a perfect match for Grazia. How could his mother think that his finals were more important than his sister's life? Ignoring his mother's pleas, he went ahead anyway.

Ushering Jens into a small, cramped office, the renal consultant could barely hide his embarrassment as he concluded, "I'm afraid the tests show that you are not a good enough match."

"How is that possible? I am her full brother." To avoid getting drawn into what was going to be a very difficult conversation with a final-year medical student, the consultant reluctantly agreed to let him see the results of tests on all family members so that he could work out for himself where the problem lay. His paternal DNA bore no relation to his father's DNA. Jens left the building in a state of total shock and drifted aimlessly around the city streets for hours, his mind in turmoil.

At least he now understood his mother's reaction to his wish to donate a kidney to his sister, but that was all he understood. His biological father was not Jan-Marten Timmerman, the only father he had ever known and the only father he would ever want. Had pregnancy been the reason his grandfather had thrown his mother out of the family home at the age of sixteen? But the dates didn't work. He was twenty-three and his mother had just had her forty-second birthday. If she had been sixteen when she left home and perhaps seventeen by the time she gave birth, that still left an unexplained gap of three years. Was she thrown out because of her lifestyle and got pregnant three years later?

He vaguely recollected hearing some story about her being held captive for four years. Did one of her captors get her pregnant? He had never asked about that—didn't even want to think about it. It belonged to his mother's past and, as all sons know, a mother's past begins on the day her son is born!

She had met Jan-Marten at university and everyone in the family knew she was pregnant when they got married. No one had ever doubted that the child was Jan-Marten's and there were photos of Jan-Marten proudly holding Jens on the day he was born. Had his mother fooled Jan-Marten into thinking Jens was his when, in fact, he was someone else's child? That seemed so unlikely.' His parents seemed far too open and honest with each other for that kind of deception. He had never doubted that his light brown hair and piercing blue eyes had been inherited from the Timmermans—the Martinez side of the family were dark-haired with olive skin. That said, the Timmermans had grey eyes, not blue eyes…

Jens thought back to the moment when he had told his parents that he intended to donate a kidney. He had been so focussed on his mother's reaction that he hadn't registered his father's response. He now recalled that his father had been staring out of a window and had said nothing. That alone told a thousand stories. They had both known what the matching process would reveal.

Did he want to know who his biological father was? No, he did not! Jan-Marten was his father. It was Jan-Marten who had read bedtime stories to him, played football with him, taught him to ride a bike, encouraged him every step of the way towards adulthood. Reluctantly, he knew he would have to speak to his parents—he didn't want to, but he had to. By now, they would know he knew, and they had enough to worry about without stressing over how this revelation might have affected him. He just needed to tell them that he loved them, that he was Jan-Marten's son in all ways that mattered, and that they could tell him more—or not—in better times once Grazia had had her transplant.

*

A donor was found, and six months later, colour returned to Grazia's cheeks and she was beginning to put on some much-needed weight. Like all junior doctors, Jens worked long hours, constantly on edge in case he missed a vital clue or misdiagnosed symptoms. He had little time to dwell on the unwelcome revelations of his lineage, but on the rare occasions when he was at home, he sensed tension in the air and an unaccustomed diffidence in the way his parents related to him. It was time to talk to his mother and she agreed, adding that she would like Jan-Marten to be there as well.

"As you know, I went off the rails in my teens and my father threw me out," Silvia began hesitantly. "I was angry at the way my father treated my mother, angry at his violent rages and at his ridiculous rules, so I rebelled, which of course only made matters worse. I hadn't a clue how to go about finding work or a place to stay, and I had no survival skills for living on the streets. I was picked up by a much older man who told me he was Pieter Steen, originally from Amsterdam. He took me to live with him on a remote estate. The only people I saw were his 'Dutch' bodyguards and the local hard men who later replaced them.

"In the early days, groups of increasingly anxious old men came to the house and retreated to discuss 'business' far into the night. Over dinner, they would speak heavily accented Spanish for my benefit, later reverting to what I thought was Dutch in conversations from which I was excluded. My only companion was my horse, Silke.

"The man I knew as Pieter was often absent. He was kind to me in his own controlling way, only occasionally wanting me in his bed—thankfully. I was only allowed out if he, or more usually his driver, accompanied me. That was my life for four years until Pieter relented and allowed me to attend a short course at university, where I met your father. Together, we discovered that Pieter was German, not Dutch, and that he was a war criminal in hiding."

Jens felt the room spin as he guessed what was coming next.

"I managed to escape and was rescued by Jan-Marten and your grandfather, only to discover that I was two months pregnant. I told Jan-Marten, and he decided that we should marry as soon as possible. We would tell his parents that I was pregnant but allow them to believe the baby was Jan-Marten's. He took the flak for getting me pregnant—things were very different in our day. Apart from you and a renal consultant, no one else knows the truth."

"The only truth that matters is that you are my father," Jens said on the verge of tears. His father gripped his hand. "Who was this other person then—I'd better know I suppose."

"His name was Hans Peter von Seidel. When he realised that I had escaped and knew who he really was, he fled before he could be captured. He was eventually arrested in Istanbul, and I believe he died in prison there."

This was so much worse than Jens had imagined. He had expected to hear the story of a one-night stand after a drink- and drug-fuelled party, or that he was the result of a brief affair with a married man. He had just heard that the genes of a Nazi war criminal coursed through his body. For the moment, he could take no more disclosure.

"That's all I need to know, for now," he said, grabbing both parents in a brief bearhug. "I just need a bit of time to digest this. I'm going for a walk to clear my head. See you later." His parents watched him go, wordlessly.

*

For the next three years, Jens worked himself to a standstill. He tried to suppress the knowledge that he had inherited a killer's genes in a whirlwind of activity inside and outside work. He knew he was becoming impossible to live with and that he was drinking too much. After months of trying to get him to tell her what was wrong, his long-term partner, Assunta, left him. Reeling from this further blow to the foundations of his life, he made a surprising decision without ever knowing why.

A boy he had been friendly with at school was now a Jesuit priest at the Iglesia de San Ignacio in Buenos Aires. Federico's sudden vocation had taken his friends by surprise. Many of his classmates were nominally Catholic, but for most, church attendance was limited to Christmas, Easter, weddings and funerals, and Federico had seemed no different. Jens had not seen him for some time. *Typical of me*, he thought, *to forget a friend until I need him*, but he could talk to a priest in confidence, and he suddenly realised that he desperately needed to talk to someone.

If Father Federico Alvarez was surprised to see Jens at evening Mass, he hid it well. Jens lingered until he was sure the last parishioner had left before moving forward to greet his friend. A huge welcoming smile lit Father Alvarez's face as he hugged Jens.

"It's wonderful to see you, Jens," he began, his smile fading as he realised tears were streaming down Jens's face. "Why don't we go up to my sitting room—it will be quieter there. I'll tell the sacristan to make sure we are not disturbed."

The Jesuit house was peaceful, smelling vaguely of incense and furniture polish. Federico led the way up a flight of stairs, pointing out a fine stain-glass window and a copy of 'The Thinker', Rodin's famous sculpture. "I keep that to remind me to do more thinking and less talking," he said, breaking the awkward silence, a compassionate smile lighting his eyes. Jens was ushered into a pleasing, book-lined room. Four comfortable chairs were arranged around a coffee table. A laptop and printer sat on a heavily carved wooden desk, and a large picture window filled the room with early evening light.

Once they were seated, Federico asked, "Would a whisky help?"

"Yes…no…well, maybe yes."

Jens watched as his friend poured two large measures from a crystal decanter. Federico placed them carefully on the coffee table, relaxed back into an armchair and released his clerical collar. "Damned uncomfortable things," he said, tossing it aside and undoing the top button of his shirt. Small, thoughtful gestures that spoke of friendship rather than formality in a way no words could have conveyed.

"Do you want to tell me what's troubling you, Jens? You know it will go no further than the walls of this room."

For Jens, the floodgates opened and he told Federico everything he had found out about his lineage and how he had tried to suppress the knowledge for three years as his private life fell apart.

"I just wish there was a way to rinse von Seidel's genes out of my body, but of course, that's not possible. I am just so scared that there is a latent capacity for evil inside me—that the whole genetics versus conditioning argument ends up favouring the genetic; that the wonderful role model that Jan-Marten has always been for me is not enough to counteract a war criminal's genes; and that one day something awful may erupt inside me."

"Jens, you are the man you were on the day before you found all this out. You are the man who wanted to donate a kidney to his sister. You are the man who chose to be a doctor when you could have earned far more if you had joined your father's law practice. You are Jan-Marten's son. This von Seidel character's influence ended with the provision of some biological material. Minute cells with no capacity to determine character. As a doctor, you know that. If it were otherwise, no one would agree to in-vitro fertilisation by donor, would they?"

Federico's thoughtful, quiet delivery had a calming effect. The first time Jens had felt calm in a very long time.

"I think I need to find out more about von Seidel—who he was and what sort of war crimes he committed. I am just scared."

"Do you think that would help—that finding out what he had done would really help? …What if the truth is awful? Won't knowing the truth just make things worse?"

"I think I have to know if I am ever going to stop this destroying me."

"There is no doubt, facing the truth can sometimes lead to healing, and maybe the mental effort of trying to deny the truth has contributed to the way you have been feeling lately. But you must be very sure before you embark on a search—sure that you are strong enough to accept hard truths."

"I have to know."

"There is just one further consideration. If von Seidel had any redeeming qualities, these are unlikely to get a mention in newspaper coverage from the time, or from court proceedings or history books. A search will not give the full picture of the man."

"If my mother's body language was anything to go by, von Seidel was decidedly short on redeeming qualities, though she tried her best to make light of it."

"Let's start the search together then," said Federico, refilling their glasses before moving over to his desk and opening the laptop.

Three hours later, the decanter was empty. In the closeness that comes from shared horror, the friends sat in silence trying to absorb what they had just learned.

*

Sharing that intensely emotional evening reignited their former friendship, and over the next two years, Jens and Federico met as often as their busy lives allowed. They seldom talked about Hans Peter von Seidel, although his ghost hovered around them at times. Federico's calm acceptance of the truth helped Jens not to define himself by it. Jens sometimes spoke of taking time out to visit some of the places in Europe and Türkiye where Hans Peter had been.

"I'm not sure that's a wonderful idea, Jens. Visiting sites of war-time atrocities, holocaust museums, or galleries displaying paintings he had once looted would be traumatic. Relatives who are currently unaware of your existence may be less than enthusiastic about meeting a son of Hans Peter. The family home, Schloss Staufensee, lay derelict for years before being bought by a luxury hotel chain and will now bear no resemblance to the place where Hans Peter was brought up. And if you go to Istanbul, what are you going to do? Stand outside a storage facility which once held Hans Peter's horde, or gaze at the courtroom where he was tried, or the prison where he died? Let it go, Jens."

*

Sleep eluded Jens that night. Federico's reaction to his idea of trying to trace Hans Peter's footsteps had prompted all sorts of doubts. He knew Federico was right. This still-vague plan had the potential to cause major upset to himself, to his parents and to any relatives he managed to trace in Germany. It could reignite supressed memories and painful truths best left buried. But this was his ancestral line, not Federico's, and no matter how supportive and understanding Federico was, it was not his history.

He reopened the file in which he had stored everything he had been able to find out about Hans Peter. It made appalling reading—the only redemptive note in the unremitting litany of evil was the fact that he had saved his mother from a desperate, self-destructive situation, although holding her captive for four years was hardly the act of a saint.

Unable to sleep, he decided to make a note of all the members of the von Seidel family mentioned in reports, however fleetingly.

- Hans Ludvig von Seidel: Bavaria. *My 'grandfather'*: Art dealer—legal and stolen. Friend of Herman Göring. Died Schloss Staufensee, 1990.
- Stefania von Seidel: Bavaria. Hans Ludvig's daughter. *My aunt*. Died 1993. No other information.
- Hans Peter von Seidel: Bavaria. Hans Ludvig's oldest son. War criminal. Murderer. Art thief. Post-war alias Pieter Steen. *My biological father*. Died Istanbul, 1998.
- Hans Dietrich von Seidel: Bavaria. Hans Ludvig's second son. Iron Cross Afrika Corps. *My uncle*. Died Berlin, 1945.
- Third son—died in childhood?
- Hans Albrecht von Seidel: Hans Ludvig's fourth son. Academic, Roman Catholic priest. *My uncle*. Murdered, Istanbul, 1991.
- Hanna Brandt: wife/partner? of Hans Dietrich. *My aunt*. Berlin. Would be in her late 90s if still alive.
- Magdalena Brandt: Born 1946. Daughter of Hanna and Hans Dietrich. Lawyer in Heidelberg. *My cousin*.
- Charles Gibson: close friend/lover? of Hans Albrecht. Murdered, Edinburgh, 1993.

All the above deceased, apart from Magdalena Brandt—Hanna Brandt an outside possibility.

He made a second list of people who might be able to tell him more about Hans Peter:

- Magdalena Brandt—internet search: possibly with Brandt und Stollenberg, law firm Heidelberg. Starting point?
- Commander Kadir Demercol: Istanbul. Arrested Hans Peter for murder and art theft, 1995. Possibly still with the Istanbul police. Old aristocratic family. Traceable?
- Chief Inspector John Arbuthnot: Scotland. Charged Hans Peter with murder of Charles Gibson. Probably retired. (Arbuthnot's name crops up in another high-profile murder case: Dr Hafez Yilmaz. Edinburgh, 1997?) No contact details. Traceable?
- Angharad (Anya) Wilson: found the ring that led to Hans Peter's arrest. No information about present whereabouts.
- Jewish Documentation Centre, Vienna.
- Museums and galleries: where to start…?

*

Father Federico Alvarez simply groaned when Jens showed him his homework a few weeks later.

"So, you have finally decided to go on this madcap venture, then?"

"I have. My maternal grandfather, General Martinez, left me enough money in his will to take a year out to go travelling."

"What do your parents think of this."

"Seriously alarmed, I think, is the best description. My ever-practical father thinks there are better things I could do with the money—like making a down payment on a house. My mother is terrified of the effect this might have on me, and of the situations I might get drawn into."

"I am with your parents on this. However, I can see that you have made up your mind—but you're surely not going to spend a whole year delving into the dark past, are you?"

"Heavens, no. I'll do Germany, Italy and Türkiye first—get that bit over, then maybe India or Australia. If I can track down John Arbuthnot, I may add UK to the list. Who knows."

"Where will you start?"

"I think I will have to start with the Brandt family in Heidelberg."

"I'll ask my Superior if I can have two weeks off to join you on part of the European tour—not the visit to the Brandts, of course. It will be difficult enough for them to discover that Hans Peter had a son with all the bad memories that may resurrect. Adding a Jesuit to the mix might just tip them over the edge."

"Thanks. It will be great to have you along to keep me from doing anything really crazy. My mother will be relieved!"

"I haven't done very well so far in keeping you from doing crazy things. The best we can hope for is that I can achieve some damage limitation. Have you set the ball rolling yet?"

"I wrote to Magdalena Brandt at the law office of Brandt & Stollenberg in Heidelberg, and I have had a rather stiff reply from her son, Dietrich Brandt-Stollenberg. He confirms that his mother is the daughter of Hanna Brandt and Hans Dietrich von Seidel, but she is not ready to see me. He has agreed to meet me at the Adlon Kempinski Hotel in Berlin—he apparently works in the Berlin office of the family firm. It was not exactly a warm letter, and the internet images of the Adlon look decidedly intimidating."

"Are you surprised?"

"No, not really."

"Let me know when the Berlin stage of your saga is over, and I'll try to get out to join you as soon as possible afterwards."

Chapter 7
Berlin 2016

Dear Federico,

I saw him at once as soon as I entered the lounge of the Adlon. Or rather, I saw a mirror image of myself as I might look in fifteen years' time. He rose to his feet as he saw me approaching, his right hand extended, "Dietrich Brandt-Stollenberg," he said briskly. A twitch of the lips was the nearest he got to a smile, which in any case did not reach the blue eyes studying me warily.

"Jens Timmerman," I replied, taking the proffered hand briefly. He sat down, crossing one elegantly clad leg across the other and continuing to stare at me.

"Good God, you look like us!" he exclaimed with a forced laugh. "Right down to the von Seidel nose!" I didn't know how to respond—the last thing on earth I want to know is that I look like my biological father.

"Forgive me," he said as he called over a waiter. "What would you like to drink?" The honest answer would have been a triple whisky, but I had a vision of your disapproving face and settled for a coffee. He did likewise with probably the same degree of reluctance.

"Your letter came as something of a shock to us," he said. I replied rather undiplomatically that it had been a shock for me too, finding out that the man I always thought was my father wasn't, and that my biological father was Hans Peter von Seidel. He remained silent and I knew that I was handling the situation badly. I was about to apologise when he started talking again.

"You will be finding this as difficult as I am, but you must understand how traumatic it was for my family following Hans Peter's arrest and trial. It was front-page news in newspapers and television across the world for weeks on end. It would subside for a time, then it would erupt again. A book would be published about the fate of a family from whom Hans Peter had stolen everything they ever valued—home, freedom, belongings; a new visitor centre would be opened at the site of one of the atrocities in which he was involved, complete with a photograph of him on the wall; or a documentary would be produced about the restoration of paintings which had been held too long in a Turkish vault; and every so often, an article would appear in Der Spiegel, or Paris Match, or Life magazine, featuring some aspect of the man's villainy.

"We never used the von Seidel name, but people knew we were related. My parents' law firm lost a third of its clients in the space of a few days. We were door-stepped by journalists outside our home. It was worse for my grandmother, who had known Hans Peter, and for my mother who is the child of Hans Peter's brother. My sister and I had a terrible time at school, Elsa more so than me. I went to Berlin two years later and fortunately no one at university made the connection, or if they did, they chose not to mention it. My sister had to endure

six years of bullying and being ostracised by friends before she could leave school and Heidelberg for good.

"Of course, Hans Peter was a monster—sorry. But there were five siblings. No one mentions Stefania, who gave everything she had and everything she could salvage from the family home to create a community for war orphans. No one mentions my grandfather, Hans Dietrich, who won an Iron Cross in Africa and was killed as the Russians rampaged through Berlin. No one mentions Hans Albrecht, who was murdered as he tried to locate Hans Peter's horde of stolen art so that all could be returned to its rightful owners.

"No one mentions family tragedies—a child who died in mysterious circumstances and a mother who died in childbirth. No one mentions my grandmother, who struggled to bring up a child on her own in war-torn, communist East Germany. Only Hans Peter. Only ever Hans Peter!"

It was only as I listened to him speak that I realised how much better you had understood the impact my sudden appearance might have on the Brandt family. They must have been terrified that I was planning to write a book, make a film, or publicise in any way my recent discovery about my biological father. I reassured Dietrich that I was as anxious as they were to keep my parentage secret. That the only people who knew were my parents, you, and the Brandt family. All that the renal surgeon in Buenos Aires knew was that my paternal DNA did not match Jan-Marten's DNA, and I was therefore not a good enough match to donate a kidney to my sister.

I asked Dietrich to apologise to his mother on my behalf, to reassure her that this was a very private and personal quest, and that the only person outside our immediate families who knew or would ever know was a Jesuit.

Dietrich suddenly relaxed and called the waiter back. "I think we both need something stronger than coffee after all this." As we waited for our drinks, he added with a giggle, "This is completely mad. I have just realised that you are my uncle! Your father was my grandfather's older brother, yet you are at least fifteen years younger than me. That would present a challenge to anyone trying to depict our family tree." We both laughed so loudly and so long that heads turned.

Dietrich has asked if I will have dinner with him the day after tomorrow and plans to drive me to Bavaria at the weekend to see the Schloss (formerly Villa) Staufensee, now a five-star-plus hotel. He says the outside is unchanged from the 'ridiculous pastiche'—his words, not mine—that his great-grandfather/my grandfather created from a fine Palladian villa. We may not get much sense of it as a family home inside though. I hope to move on from Berlin next week. Please let me know when you can get here. I need your wise head and steadying hand.

Yours ever
Jens

Chapter 8
Dinner in Berlin

As arranged, Dietrich collected Jens from his lodgings two days later.

"We shall be dining at our house this evening. I hope you don't mind, but we thought it would be more relaxing than a restaurant. It's about half an hour's drive to Charlottenburg, where we live. Hopefully, the traffic won't be too heavy."

Jens was not at all sure that dining at Dietrich's home would be relaxing. It meant gearing up to meet his wife and children who must have grave reservations about welcoming Hans Peter's son into their home. He wished Federico was with him—it had been mad to try to do this alone. The only consolation was that it would place less strain on his limited budget than dining at the kind of restaurant a man who drank in the Adlon might choose.

"Here we are," Dietrich announced as he turned into the driveway of a modern villa set well back from the main road. He parked in front of the house and Jens followed him along a path, which wound around to the back garden. A well-kept lawn stretched back to an old stone wall lined with espaliered fruit trees. An elderly couple and a younger woman sat on occasional chairs under a solitary olive tree which showed distinct signs of its struggle for survival in an alien climate. A blaze of cultivated and wildflowers tumbled over side borders and a table had been laid on a wide patio leading to open French windows.

As Jens approached, the group rose. The older woman was tall and slim with silver-grey hair swept back into a chignon. A single strand of pearls adorned her tailored blue dress. A barely perceptible smile flitted across her anxious face. The military bearing of the man beside her was softened by a brightly coloured shirt under an expensive linen jacket. His expression was both welcoming and wary. The younger woman stood slightly to the side.

Dietrich moved forward to make the introductions. "This is my mother, Magdalena Brandt." Jens felt faint—as if his legs would give way at any moment. He hadn't been expecting this—his first cousin, niece of Hans Peter, Stefania, and Albrecht. Dietrich had told him that Magdalena didn't want to meet him, and he was so taken aback that he almost missed the introductions to Herman Stollenberg, Dietrich's father, and his sister, Elsa. The conventional words of welcome did not quite match the wary expression in their eyes.

Two visibly nervous teenage girls brought out a tray of glasses and a jug of fresh fruit juice. The girls' distinctive von Seidel features were softened by inheriting much of the beauty of the woman who followed them with a platter of appetisers. Dietrich's family. His extended family.

"I can't believe you have all agreed to meet me," Jens stammered, "that you have come all the way from Heidelburg, Magdalena—and from Hamburg, Elsa? Thank you so much."

As Dietrich had known they would, his family gradually warmed to Jens—to his openness, gentle intelligence and humility. Qualities that were attributable to his mother and Jan-Marten, not to his biological father. He told them about his childhood, about his work as a doctor in a busy university hospital, his sister's illness and the trauma of discovering who his biological father was. There was no point in concealing the horror of the discovery—not even to Hans Peter's blood relatives. He listened as they described the awful aftermath of Hans Peter's arrest, the shocking disclosure of the extent of his crimes and the endless trials. Over dinner, conversation moved on to other things.

At the end of the evening, there were no false promises of continued contact—no one wanted that, but everyone was content in their own way that the evening had gone so well after an awkward start when no one had been sure that this was a good idea. Dietrich confirmed that he would take Jens to Bavaria at the weekend. After Jens had left, Dietrich's older daughter pierced the collective family tension by announcing that Jens was decidedly dishy, provoking an outburst of laughter—a welcome release.

Chapter 9
Schloss Stauffensee

On Saturday, Dietrich and Jens caught an early-morning flight to Munich. Dietrich went to pick up a hire car while Jens met Federico off a Lufthansa flight from London.

"My goodness, have you flown directly from Buenos Aires?" Dietrich asked as he loaded bags into the car. "You must be utterly exhausted."

Federico smiled. "No. I have been at the Jesuit headquarters at Mount Street in London on a mission for my Superior for the last four days. It broke the journey beautifully—with the added advantage that the Order paid for the London leg of my trip. This is my first time in Germany, and I am really looking forward to the visit."

"Well, you have come to the most beautiful part—although, as a Bavarian forced into exile in the north, I may be slightly biased. Let's get going. I know a really good restaurant on the outskirts of Munich where I can guarantee that your lunch will be better than your airline breakfast."

Federico and Jens were enthralled by the hour's drive to Rosenheim. The landscape as they approached the foothills of the Alps was so different from their native land. The burnished red and gold of the autumn colours on the lower slopes contrasting with the tall, dark green firs higher up the hillsides, and now and again, tantalising glimpses of shimmering lakes and mountain chalets. Federico apologised for his scant knowledge of the history of the area and Dietrich was only too pleased to fill in the gaps. They checked into a little three-star hotel in Rosenheim, and Jens appreciated Dietrich's sensitivity to their financial situation—he doubted if the man had ever stayed in less than a five-star hotel before.

"I suggest we drop our bags and head straight out to see the Schloss. It would be good to arrive in time to see it in daylight before the light fades. That way, we can admire it in all its pretentious grandeur in both settings. But, before we go, I must show you an old photograph of the original villa before Hans Ludwig set to work on turning it into a replica of Neuschwanstein Castle. I think he must have been as mad as his namesake King Ludwig, only much less pleasant."

The sepia photograph showed an attractive Palladian villa, surrounded by sweeping lawns and flowerbeds. An unknown couple sat in the shade of a pergola, a large wolfhound at their side staring directly at the camera.

"Hold on to that image, gentlemen!" Dietrich said with a laugh as they walked towards their car.

"Here we go," he said, twenty minutes later as he swung the car towards massive, wrought-iron gates supported on either side by mighty, ornate pillars.

"I believe the original gate was wooden and didn't shut properly," he said as a disembodied voice on an intercom invited him to identify himself. The Brandt-Stollenberg name did the trick, and the gates swung noiselessly open. The long driveway was lined with large, wrought-iron braziers and, at the final turn, Jens and Federico gasped. The lawn was still there but the old wooden pergola had been replaced by a series of kitsch, vine-covered structures promising shade and privacy to wealthy clients, not all of whom might have wanted to advertise their presence. But it was the building that left them speechless.

"You can never have too many towers and turrets, or too many balconies, weathervanes, gold domes and niches!" Dietrich observed with a laugh. "Have you ever seen anything like it?"

They hadn't. It was just about possible to make out the lines of the original villa around the grandiose entrance with its covered canopy providing shelter for fragile souls stepping down from their chauffeur-driven Mercedes or Rolls Royce. A series of semi-circular, carpeted steps led to a posse of liveried flunkies waiting in attendance at the entrance.

As the trio entered the reception area, Federico whispered, "I must be the poorest man ever to enter through the front door of this place." The others suppressed laughs as they were formally greeted by the doorman and ushered towards the lounge, where a beautifully attired waiter took their order for drinks.

"This is my treat," Dietrich said, much to the relief of his companions. Afterwards, they wandered around the hotel, mouths agape at the ostentatious luxury of everything—from the gilded dining room to the luxury spa suite. Many very fine original paintings hung on the walls, but Jens was relieved to note that they postdated anything his forebears might have 'collected'.

"All that is left from my great-grandfather's time are the huge Murano glass chandeliers and the marble floor in the main hall," Dietrich explained. "Great-Aunt Stefania sold everything she could lay her hands on to fund a community village for war orphans. I can show you the place on the way back to Rosenheim, if you like. It no longer houses orphans but still operates as a centre for children with severe disabilities."

The sun had set by the time they walked back to the car. The trio paused for a moment to gaze at the way the uplighting on the building picked out its many over-the-top features; and the braziers lining the driveway which were turning night into day.

"I find it hard to imagine my forebears living in this place—your forebears too, Jens, even if I try mentally to strip out the extravagant alterations made by its present-day Saudi owners."

Jens had no words, just a quiet satisfaction that he felt no emotional connection whatsoever to the place his biological father had called home. Federico too was silent, thinking that the receipts for twenty-four hours in that temple to excess would feed the people in a Brazilian favela for a week.

Dietrich suggested that they eat at a beer garden—a catharsis to be among ordinary people again, enjoying beer and simple food. Dietrich bade them farewell in Munich the following morning. From there, Jens and Federico planned to head south towards Bolzano in Italy.

Chapter 10
Sydney, Australia
Five Months Later

Rob and Mary Blyth were increasingly horrified at the cost of renovating their lovely Victorian terraced villa on Glebe Point Road. In the eighteen months since they had moved in, unanticipated works had included significant repairs to the decorative, wrought-iron balustrades on their first-floor balcony—a listed feature on these sought-after properties. The estimate for salvaging the ground floor from DIY structural alterations carried out—without planning permission, needless to say—by a previous owner left them with no option but to let out one of their rooms to a post-doctoral research fellow at the university where Rob was professor of anthropology.

The researcher in question was Anoushka Demercol, a graduate of Istanbul University and a delight to have around. Few paying guests would have been so relaxed about negotiating builders' rubble to get to a bathroom, or so handy with a paintbrush.

Like most young travellers in the area, Anoushka had quickly found the Toxteth Bar. She didn't drink much, at least not at the rate of some of her fellows, but she loved the buzz, the company and the tales that travellers told. She particularly liked a young Argentinian doctor called Jens who had taken a year out to do some ancestor-tracing in Europe and see a bit of the rest of the world. In fact, if she were honest with herself, her feelings for Jens ran rather deeper than simple liking. He was tall, lightly tanned and, she had to admit, in great shape. He had told her his mother was of Spanish origin, and she assumed his blue eyes and light brown hair were inherited from his Dutch/Argentinian father.

Most of all, he was fascinating to talk to and interested in her research into the anthropology and history of indigenous Australians. He was also very kind. The one thing he was reticent about was his recent ancestor search in Europe. Perhaps he had found out very little or had been disappointed in what he had uncovered. It struck her as odd that his search had not included the Netherlands or Spain, given his family background—but perhaps he already knew enough about his Dutch and Spanish forebears. When she had asked if he had made it as far as Türkiye, he had said 'yes', then abruptly closed the conversation down. Slightly taken aback, she had not pursued the matter. There was a reserve about him, a mystery behind the warm smile.

*

"Can I invite Jens to join us for supper tomorrow night?" Anoushka asked Mary Blyth. They were in the kitchen turning over a strange, official-looking package. Earlier that day, while builders had been exposing the original Victorian fireplace in the living room—a gem hidden for decades behind a flame-effect electric fire—a loose brick had fallen out. As they were replacing the brick, they noticed a package tucked down behind it and handed it over to Mary. It was wrapped in heavy brown paper with two forwarding instructions on the front, one scored out, the second dated just a few weeks before Miss Harriman's death. The first instruction read, 'In the event of my death, please return to Mr William Simpson, PO Box 5769, Fener, 50135 Istanbul, Türkiye.' This had been scored out and replaced with, 'In the event of my death, please forward to Superintendent John Arbuthnot, 8 Woodland Lane, Leigh-on-Sea, Essex, England. He will know what to do with it.'

Anoushka let out a squawk, "That's impossible! John Arbuthnot is a friend of my dad's!"

Mary stared at her in amazement. "Wait a minute, was he the British policeman who worked with your dad on that war-crime case years ago—the one that was all over the news?"

"That's the one! And they worked together on another high-profile child-trafficking case as well. Who put the envelope there, do you think?"

"I assume it was Eileen Harriman, the old lady who used to own this house."

"But why stuff the package behind the fireplace if it was so important? A new owner might have liked the electric fire—it was in good condition if you like that sort of thing—and then the package would never have been found."

"I think death caught Miss Harriman by surprise. She was apparently fit for her age and simply collapsed on the street one day. She might have intended handing the package to her lawyer before she died."

"Do you think we should open it, or just post it to John?"

"Hello, what's going on?" Rob asked as he came into the kitchen. They showed him the package. "I think we should call Miss Harriman's lawyer and ask for advice in case the contents are valuable—it might count as part of Miss Harriman's estate. I also think you should phone your dad, Anoushka, and tell him about this. We certainly shouldn't tamper with it."

The lawyer agreed to meet Mary and Anoushka the following morning.

*

At eight o'clock in the morning, on the other side of the world, John Arbuthnot was up a ladder fighting a losing battle with a large, exuberant rambling rose which his wife Anya wanted tied to a trellis. Enraged at its encroaching imprisonment, a sturdy stem broke free, driving a thorn into its assailant's arm. John let out a loud curse, unaware that his wife was standing at the foot of the ladder trying to tell him something.

"John, there's a lawyer from Sydney on the phone. He says he needs to talk to you urgently."

"A lawyer from Sydney? Are you sure he's got the right number?"

"He is quite sure and very anxious to speak to you."

Puzzled, but intrigued, John climbed down the ladder, conceding round one to the rose.

*

Mary and Anoushka were shown into the lawyer's office as soon as they arrived. Blinds filtered the strong sunlight beating down on the window from outside, casting slim beams of silver across a red oriental carpet. Bookshelves in a light wood Anoushka did not recognise lined the walls on three sides of the office. A massive, gilt-framed painting of Venice in a haze hung behind the lawyer's desk. If it was a signed copy, it was a very good one. If it was an original Turner, it was worth a fortune.

"I have taken the precaution of checking out former Superintendent Arbuthnot—an interesting man by all accounts—and called him yesterday evening, early morning UK time. I have received an email from him saying that he has been in touch with your father, Miss Demercol, and that they have agreed that you and Mary should open the package in my presence. Before we send it to Mr Arbuthnot, we need to be able to declare what it contains for customs. He has stressed that if it contains written documents, we should *not* read these, simply record that the package contains documents on the declaration form. If it contains anything of monetary value, or anything unusual, we should call him to discuss how to proceed.

"He has advised us—*instructed us*, might be more accurate—to say nothing about this to anyone else. When we have checked the contents, I am to repackage everything in a sealed envelope with our firm's official address on it, and courier it to him by the fastest means possible."

Mary carefully opened the outer packaging and found a large envelope inside.

"Those are Turkish stamps!" Anoushka exclaimed.

This envelope was addressed in a steady hand to Miss Eileen Harriman at the Glebe Point Road address. Inside, a

British government logo headed the first of five sheets of paper, all handwritten in code. There was no signature.

"Well, that saves us from the temptation of talking about the contents," the lawyer said with a laugh. "I'll get this repackaged and sent off by courier this morning."

"I'll call Dad as soon as he has woken up," Anoushka said.

*

After his phone call to Kadir, John was more puzzled than ever. He had known Eileen Harriman slightly during his time at the Met. He had been a young DS attached to a team working on a murder case which had brought the jealously guarded boundaries between the Met, MI5 and MI6 into sharp focus. An MI6 officer's mutilated body had been found in a lockup in Bermondsey. The owner of the lockup could not be traced. The victim had been recalled from Istanbul to be questioned about his links with Russian agent Oleg Peskov, at that time attached to the Russian Embassy in Ankara.

A few years earlier, agent Peskov had been expelled from UK over his part in a financial scandal involving a high-flying English banker. To say MI6 had been alarmed to discover that its man in Istanbul had been seen in the company of Peskov would have been an understatement. The agent had missed his second appointment with Eileen Harriman and had not been seen alive again. MI6 had insisted on control of a case involving one of its own—a case with potentially damaging implications for the reputation of the agency. MI5 had declared that, as the murder had occurred in London and had security implications, it was theirs to investigate. The Met had been equally determined that a crime committed on their patch was their responsibility.

Thirty-one-year-old DS Arbuthnot had found himself sitting at a table charged with inter-agency tensions, taking notes on behalf of the Met. It was the first time he had met Eileen Harriman, whose reputation as a tough negotiator was well known. John recalled a tall, sharp-featured woman, hair drawn back into a tight French roll. Her low voice, measured speech, and seemingly flawless arguments had brooked no contradiction. The meeting had broken up with no agreed conclusion about jurisdiction and insincere promises of collaboration.

She had approached John at coffee break to ask him what he made of it all. John recalled being taken aback at being addressed by this frightening woman but could no longer remember how he had replied. However, the encounter had been enough for Harriman to insist that he work with her on the case. Rumours had flown around that Harriman had fallen for the handsome young detective—a matter of considerable amusement to his colleagues, with the notable exception of his DCI who thought he should have been the person to liaise with Harriman.

Needless to say, there had been rather more to Harriman's selection of John than an out-of-character mid-life crush. With the young DS at her side, no one could accuse her of not collaborating with the Met, while keeping the status differential firmly in MI6's favour. By collaborating with the Met, she had eased MI5 to the sidelines—just where she liked that agency to be. She had also worked out that John was infinitely brighter than his boss. And a bright man was what she needed on this case.

Back at the crime scene, she had turned to John and asked again what he made of it all. This time, he had been ready to reply.

"The pathology report tells us that he was tortured—presumably to gain information—and strangled, but that the mutilation was carried out postmortem. As I see it, there are three agencies who might have wanted to silence him, but none of these would have had reason to mutilate his body. The Russians would have beaten him up until he told them whatever they wanted to know, then killed him—probably by lethal injection. They would have departed the scene, leaving no forensic trace.

"He might have crossed a line in Turkey and come to the attention of MIT—Turkish Intelligence. I think MIT is the least likely culprit; besides, they would have gone about the task of extracting information in the same way as the Russians—no messy postmortem mutilation. It could have been MI6, anxious to avoid damaging publicity…" John remembered hesitating at that point, wilting under Harriman's uncompromising stare, but had been invited to continue. There had been no going back.

"But I would rule out MI6. They would have made a much neater job of it and the body would simply have disappeared. This case has the hallmark of a falling-out in the organised criminal fraternity. Could our man have been involved in drug trafficking or people trafficking, for example—with or without the involvement of Peskov? More likely without, given that Peskov is still alive, still at the Russian Embassy in Ankara and still in possession of all his limbs—as far as we know. But you say there is no evidence of involvement in crime. That leaves us with the three most likely reasons for mutilating a body after death: to disfigure the body to prevent identification. Our man was not disfigured. To make it easier to remove the body. Our man was left where he died. Rage… Or…"

"Or what?" Harriman had asked.

"Or some agency wanted this to look as if it had been committed by criminals in revenge for a deal gone wrong."

John remembered Harriman staring at him for a long time before answering, "You are sharp, John. I think we might want to recruit you."

He had been stunned by the proposal, embarrassed and pleased in equal measure, but had known that moving to a job involving risk and frequent, unexplained absences from home would do nothing to mend the cracks already appearing in his marriage. Cracks that had everything to do with his unpredictable hours and occasional failure to turn up for important events with family and friends.

The case had eventually been archived. Murder by persons unknown. The victim's wife had gone to the press to complain that her husband's death had not been properly investigated. She had been invited to a meeting with Eileen Harriman. Shortly afterwards, she had gone away quietly to face widowhood with the trace of a smile.

Jolting himself back to the present, John vaguely recalled that Eileen Harriman had been forced to resign or retire early from MI6. Many years had passed since then. He had returned to Scotland after his first wife left him for a schoolteacher with regular working hours. He had not known Eileen's former colleague, William Simpson, who, he had just learned, had spent the rest of his life looking for spies in Istanbul before dying in circumstances that were less than straightforward. Now, Eileen too was dead. Coincidence?

The documents she had left for him had originally been sent from Istanbul and were apparently in code—but there was no indication as to whether the code was referenced to Turkish or English. He was sure Kadir would have access to a Turkish code-breaker, but in case an English-speaking code-breaker was needed, he would make copies of the documents and leave them with his wife, Anya. He was reluctant to take them to MI6 until he knew more about why Simpson had sent them to Harriman for safekeeping, and why Harriman had forwarded the package to him rather than to her former employer.

"It seems I am not the only woman who has found you irresistible," Anya said with a laugh. John leant forward to give her a playful kiss—a kiss which suddenly developed into something more urgent.

"The rose, John!" Anya said, pulling away gently.

"A postponement then," John replied with a knowing smile. "A reward for injuries sustained while fighting a rose on behalf of my lady."

"The enemy awaits," Anya replied, pointing to the garden door and handing him the secateurs and twine.

*

The Express courier promised delivery within forty-eight hours, on which basis John booked a flight to Istanbul three days hence. Anya had been less than amused when he told her. She was looking forward to singing in a performance of the *Christmas Oratorio* at the Albert Hall and had no intention of missing final rehearsals or the concert to sit twiddling her thumbs in Istanbul while John and Kadir played at cops and spies!

John booked a flight for her the day after her concert and attempted to conceal his relief at not having to sit through the performance. He loved Anya dearly, but their tastes in music could not have been more different. She had proved as resistant to Fleetwood Mac as he to Bach.

Chapter 11
Fenez, Istanbul

James offered to cook dinner for Ester. He wanted to talk to her on his territory, not hers. There seemed little risk in letting her know where he lived as MIT would have no difficulty in finding the address, should she ever want to know. She arrived promptly, dressed for seduction in a shimmering red silk dress, which clung in all the right places, and Jimmy Choo shoes with impossibly high heels accentuating her slim ankles. A gold and diamond necklace completed her breathtaking outfit. She accepted the proffered glass of sparkling wine and settled in a chair, from which James would have an optimum view of her beautifully shaped legs.

Once again, they talked of inconsequential things until the first two courses had been served.

"You are an excellent cook, James."

"Thank you. It is amazing how many skills a man learns when he finds himself living alone." After a pause, James continued, "Perhaps it is time to talk about the elephant in the room." Noting the puzzled look on Ester's face, he realised that excellent though her English was, the idiom of the elephant was lost on her.

"About Bill Simpson, I mean. What was he really looking for and why the recent, unlikely friendship with you?"

"He was looking for a British man spying for the Russians—the sixth man, as he called him. I found Bill amusing and vaguely ridiculous at the same time."

"I know he had Harry Haversham-Hopkiss in his sights—a friend of yours, I believe. I cannot think why Bill was still on the trail of Harry. At least forty years have passed, the world changed out of recognition, since Harry had anything of interest to pass to the Russians. I believe his former contact, Oleg Peskov, is spending his twilight years at a dacha overlooking the Black Sea, grieving for his son, Igor, who—if my information is correct—died rather unexpectedly in this very city three years ago. Another friend of yours, I am told."

Ester stared at James in a mixture of alarm and anger. Her host was far too well-informed for comfort. Who was this man? Why was he in Istanbul? Why had she made the mistake of assuming he was just another Bill Simpson on the trail of ghosts from the Cold War? She had dangerously underestimated him—a serious mistake, and Ester could not afford to make mistakes.

As the silence prolonged, James picked up the thread again, "What doesn't make sense to me is that Bill would have been aware that even if he did identify a sixth man, the British Establishment would have no interest whatsoever in raking over long-dead coals. So, I am left to wonder what Bill was really up to. Had the Peskov trail uncovered leads to something inimical to British interests—some lead to MIT, for example? If that were the case, I can understand why he wanted to get close to you.

"What I find harder to understand is why you put up with him, unless it was to find out what he knew. Well, he is dead now, so we may never find out what he may have uncovered—unless you already know, of course."

"I have no idea what you are talking about," Ester replied, hoping that her voice did not betray the icy chill of fear gripping her. Who was this man smiling provocatively at her? How much did he know? Had he guessed that Simpson's latter-day search had been focussed on her rather than on Turkish intelligence or Turkish allegiances? "Simpson was delusional, but a man better kept close than left to run amok." Even to her own ears, Ester's response sounded defensive and unconvincing.

"He also had a friend at the Russian Consulate General—any idea what that was about?"

"Sex, I should imagine!" Ester spoke more sharply than she intended.

"Sex. Hmm. I am not so sure. I have met the woman—beautiful and in her late twenties. Istanbul is full of good-looking young men, so why waste time on an Englishman well past his sell-by date? I imagine that you know her mother is the politician, Irina Peskova—Igor's sister."

Enjoying the look of horror on Ester's face, he continued, "But perhaps not, as her surname follows Russian tradition, deriving from that of her father, Andrei Stolypin—hence Katerina Stolypina, as you would know her."

Struggling for self-control, Ester responded icily, "I think we need to change the subject if we are to enjoy the rest of this evening together." Inwardly, she was seething. MIT should have known this—but then, a young cultural attaché at the Russian Consulate would have been of little interest to

MIT. But the Peskov link was of vital interest to Ester Kalik. Her very survival could depend on what that young attaché knew and what she had already done, or intended to do with any compromising data she might have uncovered. It would not be the first time that the designation, *cultural attaché*, had been used as a cover for intelligence-gathering.

James seized the moment to go into the kitchen to prepare dessert. As he began to slice into a pineapple, he sensed movement behind him. Hand clasped firmly on the knife, he turned slowly to face Ester. To his surprise, she leant forward and kissed him, open-mouthed, the tip of her tongue trailing lightly on his lips. His response was immediate, and she felt him harden against her. She had just begun to congratulate herself on the success of this move, when James stepped back abruptly, hands firmly on her shoulders.

"I don't think this is a good idea, Ester. Let's take our pineapple back to the table and relax over some delicious dessert wine. I apologise for being such a brute."

Flushed with anger and shame, Ester retreated to the dining room, almost more annoyed with him for pretending he had initiated the advance than for rejecting her. Ignoring dessert, she swept up her jacket and handbag.

"Thank you for dinner, but I need to leave now." She made for the main door.

"Allow me at least to accompany you to your car."

"If you wish," she called over her shoulder as she headed out of the apartment. The man infuriated and scared her in equal measure. She had found out where and when Bill Simpson had met the Russian woman, had checked her official status at the Russian Consulate General, but *why* had she not checked her background? Another Peskov in Istanbul was very bad news indeed. Was leading a double life finally taking its toll? Was she losing her grip, fear of being unmasked clouding her judgment?

Chapter 12
Dinner at Glebe Point Road

Jens arrived promptly at Glebe Point Road and Anoushka noticed the effort he had made—the crisp white shirt, linen jacket, new jeans and large bunch of flowers.

"Jens Timmerman; thank you for inviting me," he said as he shook Rob's outstretched hand. Anoushka experienced a moment of mild surprise. One of the features of the transient Toxteth crowd was that they used first names only. She already knew … or at least hoped, that her friendship with Jens was anything but transient, and she was taken aback to realise that she hadn't known his surname.

Over drinks, Jens asked Anoushka what she had been doing that day—it wasn't a pointed question, just a slightly awkward attempt at conversation. Anoushka looked at Mary, who chipped in, "We can't really tell you very much, but workmen found a package concealed behind the fireplace in the living room with a forwarding address on it. We think the package must have been hidden there by Miss Harriman, who was the former owner of this house. In the event of her death, it was to be forwarded to a British policeman, John Arbuthnot, but Rob thought we should take it to Miss Harriman's lawyer first. We knew who her lawyer was because he dealt with the sale of the house. So, a visit to the lawyer was this morning's excitement for Anoushka and me."

"The reason I went with Mary was—and you'll never believe this—John Arbuthnot is a friend of Dad's. How about that for a coincidence?"

"Wow! That's just amazing! But why go to the expense of forwarding it through a lawyer instead of just posting it?"

Rob picked up the thread, "We thought the package looked as if it might contain official documents—many years ago, Miss Harriman worked for British Intelligence."

Anoushka and Mary looked at Rob in surprise. "You never mentioned that, Rob—about her working for British Intelligence," Mary said rather sharply.

"I thought you knew, Mary. Sorry. It was the talk of the faculty common room when she died, but of course, that was before we knew we would end up buying her house. One of my colleagues knew her—went to the same church, if I remember rightly. I don't think anyone took his conspiracy theories seriously, but the discovery of this package has made me wonder if there might have been something in his suspicions. Miss Harriman's death is officially recorded as due to natural causes, but social media was rife at the time with rumours that she might have been murdered. I believe the police investigated the rumours and concluded that they were unfounded. That is why I thought it best to deal with the package as if it were part of her estate."

"Makes sense. But what an amazing coincidence that this Arbuthnot fellow is a friend of your family, Anoushka." For some reason, the name was ringing bells for Jens.

"Let's eat," Mary said to general relief and approval.

Changing the subject completely, Jens asked, "What made you decide to carry out research into the indigenous people of Australia, Anoushka? There is so little to go on compared to Türkiye, where there are traces of human habitation stretching back thousands of years."

"It is true. The history of the land we now know as Türkiye has been explored to exhaustion by generations of Jewish, Persian, Greek, Roman, Turkish, European and Arabic scholars. Not to mention the present-day blight of American academics from little-known universities scouring the land with their film crews to make badly researched documentaries to entertain the folks back home. Plenty has been written about emperors and sultans, grand palaces, mosques, monuments and cathedrals, soldiers, battles and land grabs, but not about the lives of ordinary people.

"There may be a record of how many people died building Aya Sofia or Sinan's great mosques, but not their names or what happened to their wives and children afterwards. There is plenty written about Suleiman the Magnificent's advance towards the outskirts of Vienna, but nothing of the terrified people whose towns and villages lay in his path, people who had no idea who he was or why all the destruction in his wake. It was John Arbuthnot's wife, Anya, who taught me to sit still in places and listen to the voices of ordinary people from the past."

She was unaware of Jens stiffening at the mention of Anya Arbuthnot, as he recalled why the Arbuthnot name rang a bell. He had first encountered it in Federico's study as they scoured news coverage from the time of Hans Peter's arrest and trial.

"This is why I am so interested in people who lived lightly on the land, who built no grandiose monuments, who left no written word as we would know it—but plenty of signs and symbols if you know where to look and how to interpret these. People to whom the concept of owning the earth is completely alien."

"Your own family has quite a history," Mary commented. "Has anyone written about it?"

"Written about the Demercol family? Not as such, but generations of Demercol Generals, Admirals and Grand Viziers appear in histories from the time of the Fall of Constantinople to the present day. There is no need for anyone to write more about us—what is already documented is more than enough!" Anoushka replied with a dismissive laugh.

"Demercol. Is that your family name?" Jens asked in a strained voice.

"Yes. But my parents decided to buck the family pattern of living on past glory and privilege. Dad is a detective, and Mum still organises a food kitchen at the local mosque, to my grandmother's horror. My parents have always encouraged us to follow our own paths. My brother is an agronomist with FAO and my sister works for the UN in Switzerland…is something the matter, Jens?"

"No. No, I'm fine."

Jens was far from feeling fine. He had just realised how much he loved this woman, only to discover she was the daughter of the policeman who had arrested his biological father. He wanted to scream in impotent rage. His genetic heritage would in all possibility destroy any chance of having Anoushka beside him for life.

At the end of the evening, Jens hugged her fiercely as if it were for the last time, then ran back up Glebe Point Road to his lodgings. In the following days, he did not appear at the

Toxteth. His brief responses to Anoushka's texts were noncommittal and Anoushka couldn't work out what had suddenly gone wrong. Was it something to do with her background, or something she had said? Whatever it was, she had to find out. On the day before she had to leave for a field trip in the outback, she sent a final text, '*Please* can I see you before I go?'

'Yes, but not in the Toxteth. Can we meet in Victoria Park? I'll be waiting outside the main university building when you finish today.'

'Yes, of course. See you then.'

She sensed he was tense the moment she saw him. As they walked down the path, he stopped suddenly.

"You know I love you very much, Anoushka. More than I can possibly say, but we can't take this any further."

Anoushka burst into tears, her whole world collapsing. "But why? Is there someone else—someone waiting in Argentina?

"No. Nothing like that. It is because your father could never accept me as your boyfriend, let alone as your husband."

"Why? That makes no sense. Do you think it's because you are Argentinian, or because your family is Christian? What difference does any of that make? My family isn't racist or prejudiced."

"No. That's not the reason. Let's sit on this bench. I owe you an explanation."

"Yes, you do!" she retorted as she fumbled for a handkerchief.

"You know I told you that my parents are Argentinian— my mother Spanish, my father of Dutch descent. And that is true. Jan-Marten is the best father anyone could ever wish for. He has been with Mum since before I was born, and he is the only father I will ever acknowledge—but he is not my biological father. My problem—our problem—is that my biological father is Hans Peter von Seidel."

Hearing Anoushka gasp, he rushed on, words tumbling out, "Yes. The Nazi war criminal, art thief, and serial murderer who was finally caught by John Arbuthnot and your father. It won't matter that I thankfully never met the monster, your father would always worry that some part of him lurks inside me. I didn't tell you anything about my ancestry search because, although the relatives I met in Germany are fine people, everything I found out about Hans Peter sickened me. I wish I had never started the search—wish I had just come straight to Australia. But the truth is out now, and your father would always look at me and fear for your safety."

"Jens, you are not that man. You are the lovely man I want to spend the rest of my life with. The man who was brought up by two loving parents. The man I love. Dad will just have to get over it!"

They bought a bottle of wine and took it to Jens's room—and didn't get around to drinking it. Instead, they made love in the fierce, desperate way of people who know the path ahead will not be easy.

Chapter 13
Istanbul

John Arbuthnot arrived in Istanbul on a cold, wet evening to be met by an exuberant Kadir.

"We've cracked the code in Simpson's papers, and you will never guess what they reveal!"

John groaned inwardly. In normal circumstances, he would have preferred Kadir to concentrate on driving through the heavy rush-hour traffic on the motorway from the international airport, rather than on conversation with the speedometer registering 120k an hour. On this occasion, fear of colliding with a lumbering juggernaut was subsumed by the greater fear of what Kadir was about to disclose.

Before leaving UK, he had been called to an off-the-record meeting with the DG of MI6 and informed that an MI6 officer was on a covert mission to investigate Bill Simpson's death. He was to contact this James Davidson as soon as he arrived in Istanbul and be advised by him. The message had been clear—this was not a case for a former policeman, however highly regarded, familiar with Istanbul, and on friendly terms with the commander of the Istanbul Serious Crimes Directorate.

He just hoped that whatever Kadir had found would not result in front-page headlines to the detriment of Her Majesty's Government or the British Intelligence Services.

"Bill Simpson's code was based on Turkish and proved surprisingly easy to crack. Took our analysts less than a day. I can give you a full translation when we get home, but in brief, it catalogues Simpson's ten-year hunt for the man he believed was a sixth Cambridge spy—Harry Haversham-Hopkiss. His hypothesis was based on Harry's association with Oleg Peskov and with Oleg's son, Igor; on Harry's sudden change of fortunes after glasnost; on Harry's journey to Ankara five years earlier, which just happened to coincide with Oleg Peskov's presence in the capital. Ten years on, having found nothing more to support his conspiracy theory, he appears to have abandoned the search.

"But here is where it becomes really interesting…" Kadir paused to swerve abruptly out of the path of a slow-moving car. John realised his knuckles had gone white.

"Simpson found a new obsession! One that interests us infinitely more than it will interest you. Igor Peskov was murdered in Istanbul four years ago and Simpson got it into his head that a senior Turkish intelligence officer was responsible, whether by dealing the fatal blow or simply orchestrating it. The MIT officer he blames is none other than Ester Kalik…"

John exhaled sharply. Ester Kalik's name was widely known in international intelligence circles. He had heard her variously described as shrewd, ruthless, difficult to fathom, cooperative and obstructive in equal measure—all qualities that go with the job.

"Igor Peskov was her lover, and she was the last person to see him alive—apart from his killer, of course, unless we are talking about one and the same person. His murder remains unsolved. Simpson's theory is that Igor Peskov had some sort of hold over her and he decided to establish a relationship with Kalik to see what more he could unearth. To cap it all, he was simultaneously wining and dining Katerina Stolypina, cultural attaché at the Russian Consulate General and—wait for it—niece of Igor Peskov—presumably in the hope of finding out what kind of a hold Igor had over Kalik."

"If someone had a hold over a senior MIT officer, I can see why that would interest you, but I cannot think why it was of any interest to Bill Simpson."

"We have asked ourselves the same question, and the only thread we find in Simpson's coded text is a reference to Ester Kalik and Harry Haversham-Hopkiss being close friends—not lovers. Harry's romantic interests lie in a different direction. It seems that Simpson thought he might be back on the trail of his sixth man."

"Could this be what cost him his life?" John asked.

"It could very well be. His murder bore remarkable similarities to Igor Peskov's and Ester Kalik is the common denominator. However, if we are looking for a motive for Simpson's death, it is more likely to concern whatever Kalik feared he may have found out about her, than anything to do with Harry Hopkiss. This is the first real lead we have had on either murder."

"You will need to be on very solid ground before you interview someone like Ester Kalik," John observed thoughtfully.

"You are not wrong! MIT will not appreciate one of their senior officers being dragged into a police investigation," Kadir replied as he swung into the drive leading up to the Demercol villa. John visibly relaxed, his near-death experience over for the time being—reinvigorated by the prospect of downing a stiff drink and hugging Kadir's wife. Not necessarily in that order.

Over dinner, John asked how their youngest daughter, Anoushka, was enjoying her time in Australia and caught the look that passed between her parents.

"She is having a great time, it would seem. Her research is going well and there is a new and apparently serious boyfriend. We don't know much about him apart from the fact that he is a doctor on some sort of sabbatical. Rather ominously, she has said they would like to talk to us face to face about the relationship. So, we have no idea what lies in wait for us. Hopefully nothing worse than that he is Australian, and our youngest daughter could end up living on the opposite side of the world. Two weeks ago, we would have said that was the worst thing that could happen. Now, our imaginations are running riot."

"Anoushka is a sensible woman. If she loves this man, there can't be much wrong with him," John said, trying to lighten the mood.

*

At 2 am, James Davidson woke with a start. It had taken a long time for him to fall asleep after the strange events of the evening before, not least the lingering aftereffects of Ester's seduction attempt and the whiskies he had consumed subsequently to dull the frustration of having had to decline the offer. The insistent clamour of his telephone finally cut through the mental fog, and he fumbled around to locate his phone and see who was calling. The DG! How was it possible that the DG of MI6 was unaware of the time difference between London and Istanbul?

"Thought you'd never pick up, Davidson."

"It's halfway through the night here!"

"Ours is a service that never sleeps—hope you are not getting too old to hack it." James did not respond to the chuckle at the other end of the phone.

"Strange turn-up for the books. Seems that Harriman left instructions for a package she had been holding for Simpson to be forwarded to a former superintendent with Lothian and Borders Police, John Arbuthnot. You may know him or at least have heard of him. Are you with me so far, Davidson?"

"Just about. And yes, I have heard of him. Starring role in the capture of a Nazi war criminal, if I recall correctly. Never met him though."

"Turns out Simpson's package contained a coded report. Unfortunately, the code is based on Turkish so it will take a while to get it decoded and translated here. Arbuthnot tells me the Turks have already decoded it. That makes me very anxious. It is currently in the hands of Commander Kadir Demercol, whom I believe you have already met. Arbuthnot is staying at the Demercol villa, and I need you to get alongside him first thing this morning. You are to make sure Arbuthnot understands the need to bury anything in Simpson's report that might cause difficulty to HMG or to us."

"And if the Turks refuse to bury something that we do not like…?"

"It is your job to ensure that they don't refuse. Goodnight, Davidson."

James collapsed back on his pillows, all hope of getting back to sleep gone. This mission was assuming nightmarish proportions. One thing was certain—Commander Demercol would not bury information to spare the blushes of HMG unless it suited him to do so.

Chapter 14
Istanbul 36 Hours Later

Ester sensed the atmosphere as soon as she entered the office. Colleagues hurried past without a word, or sat hunched over computer screens or smartphones, eyes averted. Her secretary was nowhere to be seen. Her heart missed a beat at the sound of her phone ringing as she closed the door to her private office. It was her contact at police headquarters, calling from a busy café given the background noise.

"Something's up, Ester. Seems the police have found a report written by your erstwhile friend, Mr Simpson. I don't know what is in it, but I can tell you this—your boss stormed into police HQ this morning looking fit to be tied! He is currently in a meeting with Commander Demercol and two other men—foreigners I think, possibly British. I can't tell you anything more. I need to get back before anyone notices I am missing. Don't call me."

Ester's hands shook uncontrollably as she stared at her now silent phone. It could only mean one thing—Simpson had found out who she really was and, to make matters worse, his report had fallen into the hands of the police, not MIT. If the report had come directly to MIT, she might have been able to intercept it before anyone else knew about it. How many heads would roll in MIT when it became known that their second-in-command was an active member of a powerful, clandestine Palestinian organisation—designated as a terrorist organisation by Türkiye and many other nations!

With as much dignity as she could muster, Ester left her office and walked briskly past rows of silent, hostile colleagues and out into the busy world. For several hours, she wandered through backstreets, trying to work out what to do. She needed to leave the country, but border controls would already be on the lookout for her. Reluctantly, she took the SIM card out of her phone and threw it down a drain. There was a burner phone at her flat. She would use that to contact a friend who might be able to get her through the leaky border with Syria.

Where to lie low in the meantime? That was a problem. Briefly, she thought about Harry Hopkiss, but equally quickly rejected the idea. Although Harry fully understood her sympathy with the Palestinian cause, he knew nothing about her active involvement. There was no way of knowing how he would react to finding out; besides, Harry's days of high-stakes intrigue were long gone.

As the light faded, Ester watched her apartment block from a safe distance until she was sure the coast was clear. Even then, she waited until darkness had fallen before moving towards the main door. Inside the building, all was quiet as she climbed the stairs to the second floor. The door to her apartment was unlocked and she opened it cautiously. The place had been turned over very professionally. The only items taken were her laptop, passport, the contents of a filing cabinet, and the burner phone. She didn't need anyone to tell her that this was the work of MIT.

Early next morning, a nearby stall-holder would tell the police he had seen her leave in her car the previous evening. Destination unknown.

*

Six months later, a partially clothed woman's body was found in a shallow grave on the Anatolian plateau near the Neolithic site at Çatalhöyük. The remains had been disturbed by an animal. The woman was middle-aged with dyed red hair, broken teeth, missing fingernails and multiple fractures. No personal items were found in the grave. No one knew who she was. An MIT officer advised the local police that they should focus on their local priorities, and the case was closed.

*

Harry Hopkiss was devastated to learn that Ester had vanished into thin air. When his enquiries hit brick wall after brick wall, he suspected the worst, but did not have the courage or know-how to investigate further. Neither Andy McPherson at the Consulate nor that strange Englishman, James Davidson, had been able to help. He hoped she was safely back in Palestine but knew in his heart of hearts that she was not. On a rare evening out with friends, he suffered a massive coronary and died of entirely natural causes in hospital later that night.

*

Bill Simpson had died without knowing that he had been right all along. Many years earlier, a sixth man had been operating as a double agent in Istanbul—only it wasn't Harry Haversham-Hopkiss—born in war-torn Germany, parents unknown, loyalties conflicted—but a rogue MI6 officer who had died badly in a disused lockup in Bermondsey. He had been right about Ester Kalik too.

*

James Davidson's mission was over. Anything that might embarrass HMG or the British Intelligence Services had been buried with Bill Simpson. Simpson had been unable to prove that a sixth man had existed. Simpson had found no trace of a rogue MI6 officer operating in Istanbul in the years immediately preceding his own arrival in the city. Eileen Harriman had played those cards very close to her chest, trusting a young DS from the Met with a secret withheld from her colleagues.

James Davidson's task had been to ensure that the long-dead double agent's existence would remain as well and truly buried as the man himself. Simpson's more accurate revelations about a prominent Turkish citizen of Palestinian origin were for the Turkish authorities to deal with.

*

The Demercol Villa

Anya arrived in Istanbul, still on a high after a well-received performance of the *Christmas Oratorio*.

"Even the *Times* music critic had only good things to say about us and you know how devastating his judgement can be if a performance is below standard."

Smiling indulgently, Anya's current audience, though unfamiliar with the heights of excellence demanded by the *Times* music critic, shared in the euphoria of the moment. The two couples were just glad to be together, glad that a strange report written by a former British intelligence officer had given them an unexpected opportunity to spend time with each other. Time that, for once, would not be ruined by the men's involvement in high-risk police work.

Or so they thought, as they relaxed in the villa's comfortable drawing room overlooking the dark waters of the Bosphorus and the lights of passing ships shimmering through the rain. The peace was suddenly shattered by the strident ring of Kadir's phone. He whipped it out of his pocket, saw a foreign number and was about to switch the phone off when he heard the voice at the other end of the line. His face went white and conversation in the room went silent as three anxious faces turned in his direction.

Chapter 15
The Australian Outback

Anoushka and four research fellows from Sydney University had spent a productive week working their way along a song line near Broken Ridge. Their guide and unofficial leader was a brilliant indigenous Australian called Hal, whose ability to read the land and the signs left by people who had passed that way in earlier times helped the team see things they would otherwise have missed. They had risen at dawn each day and worked until the heat became unbearable towards mid-day, resuming their research again late afternoon.

In the evenings, Hal reminisced about the life and beliefs of his forebears, the creation stories passed from one generation to another, and their love of the land. He talked of their art—their wonderful depictions of wildlife and what it all meant. At other times, he spoke bitterly about the impact European immigration had had on a millennial way of life.

The final morning was spent loading their equipment into the offroad vehicles the team had driven out from Sydney—one belonging to the university and the other hired from a rental company. Anoushka packed her photographic gear into her own Toyota Rav. The intention was to drive back to Sydney in convoy, but Anoushka wanted to take a few more photographs and said she would catch up with the others on the road.

"I'll overtake your lumbering wagons halfway to Sydney," she jested.

"Would you like me to hang back with you?" Hal asked. "Just in case anything goes wrong."

"What could possibly go wrong, Hal?" She laughed. "I'll be fine on my own."

Hal said nothing. City-dwellers seldom took the dangers of the outback seriously enough. However, Anoushka seemed determined, and he reluctantly decided not to insist in case she mistook his intentions. She was only going to take a few photographs, after all, he tried to reassure himself. Twelve hours later, he would regret giving in so readily.

The morning light was a photographer's dream. Rolling folds of ochre landscape peppered with jagged rocks and, here and there, a struggling bush throwing desiccated arms upwards in supplication to an unforgiving sky. Anoushka clambered up towards a rock that had caught the team's attention earlier in the week because of the strange markings on it—markings that Hal had not recognised, and the team had lost interest. However, Anoushka wanted to do some further research on the markings before dismissing them as the work of some latter-day traveller.

She became so engrossed in her work that she lost all sense of time, and it was only as she packed her camera away that she realised how high the sun had risen, draining all colour from the sky, and how oppressive the heat had become. By the time she reached her car, she was drenched in sweat and her water bottle was almost empty.

I need to call the others and let them know I'll be late, she thought as she opened her car door—then remembered there was no signal in the area and the satellite phone was in one of the other vehicles. The inside of her car was like an oven, and she could barely touch the steering wheel, so she let the aircon run for a while before venturing inside. She was now very late.

There were two tracks leading from their former campsite to the main road, one much longer and less rugged than the other. Her car had four-wheel drive but a lower wheelbase than the offroad vehicles. For that reason, she had taken the longer track when she arrived. She decided to risk the shorter track to save time but had not made much progress before realising that this was a mistake. The track was steep and deeply rutted and it was a long time since anyone had thought to clear the boulders littering the way.

She decided to reverse back up the track and take the longer route. As she did so, the hazard warning was almost continuous. Reversing up the steep hill, she discovered how poor her sightlines were. All her rearview mirror revealed was a vast expanse of sky, and the wing mirrors showed the track to the side of her car, not the all-important track to the rear. Suddenly, a sickening and prolonged crunch on the undercarriage was followed by a blaze of warning lights on the dashboard terminating in a flashing command to stop the car and switch off the engine immediately.

Anoushka burst into tears. Nothing in her sheltered life had prepared her for this and she bitterly regretted not accepting Hal's offer to accompany her. Tears were not going to solve her desperate situation though and she quickly pulled herself together. Her only option was to walk the 5 kilometres down to the main road and hope to flag down a passing motorist. The only question was whether to shelter behind the car until the worst of the heat had passed or to set off at once.

With so little water left, she decided to go at once and to risk the steep track on foot. She made it to the main road by late afternoon, seriously dehydrated, scratched and bruised from falls on the way, dizzy, sunburnt, and with a pounding head. After what seemed like an infinity, a battered truck pulled up beside her and the driver asked if she needed help. At any other time, she would have run a mile from this driver. He was dirty and unkempt, his skin a patchwork of dark and pale blotches. His hair, teeth and nails needed serious attention—a wash would have been a good start—but Anoushka was desperate. She asked for water, and he handed her a bottle from which he had clearly been drinking. In normal circumstances, she would have gagged at the thought of touching it, but she was so thirsty that all thought of contamination fled.

"Where are you bound for, Miss?" the driver asked.

"Sydney," she replied. Noting his look of surprise, she added, "My car has broken down 5 kilometres up that track. My friends are up ahead in another vehicle, but I have no way of contacting them."

"Hop in. I can take you part of the way. Get you out of this heat for a while, at least."

Anoushka knew it was a mistake but just to get out of the sun for a while made the risk seem worthwhile. Used to the long, hot summers of Istanbul, she had naively believed she knew about surviving in intense heat, but the heat of the Australian Outback was like nothing she had ever known. She would ask to be let out as soon as the worst heat of the day had passed and wait for a better lift to Sydney.

"Where are your friends then?" the driver asked. A knowing grin spread across his face.

"Oh, just up the road a bit. They'll turn back as soon as they realise that I am not following."

"Let's see if we can catch up with them then," the driver said with a laugh and accelerated, causing his old truck to rattle and shake alarmingly.

"I'd like to get out now," Anoushka said. "It's cooler outside and I can wait for my friends to come back for me."

"You reckon. Still too hot to stand at the roadside and you don't want to get caught out here in the dark. Not with dingoes and vultures around."

"I have been working here for two weeks and so far, I have yet to see a dingo, let alone a vulture, only the moon and the stars! So, please let me out."

The driver did not respond, just pushed the accelerator hard to the floor.

"Please!"

"Can't let you out yet. Too dangerous for a young woman alone."

Anoushka leant back, head swimming, praying that this nightmare would end soon. She was shaken alert as the car made an abrupt turn off the main road.

"Stop! What are you doing? Let me out. This is not the way to Sydney. Let me out, I tell you!"

A sharp blow across her face was followed by the threat of another if she didn't 'shut the fuck up'. The truck was going too fast for her to jump out and she realised that even if she did, by the time she got back on her feet and started running, he would be after her. He wasn't old and, despite his filthy appearance, he looked fit. She had never been good at running. Hard as she tried to fight down panic, the awfulness of her situation was overwhelming all rational thought.

*

Amos was not sure what he was doing. This was not a novel situation. Amos was rarely sure of anything. He had been raised—if you could call it that—in a series of foster homes, but none of the placements had been a success. His records showed he was part indigenous and part white, abandoned at birth in Darwin. He was constantly bullied because of a rare pigmentation disorder and compensated for this with his fists. He had been expelled from every school he had ever attended, finally running away from both school and social services at the age of fourteen, barely able to read or write. Finally, at the age of twenty-five, he had taken illegal possession of an abandoned shack in the outback and survived by doing odd jobs on building sites and farms.

He hadn't meant to capture this foreign woman, but as he drove, the idea of kidnapping her for a ransom slowly took hold. He had seen a film once about a kidnap and what you did was to call the victim's family and demand a ransom. The family dropped the ransom money somewhere chosen by you, and once you checked it, you let the victim go. There was a long-abandoned mailbox at the turn-off from the main road. An ideal place for the money to be dropped.

All he needed to do was persuade the woman to come into his house where she could phone her husband or father and ask for a ransom of… what?…$50,000? $100.000 would be better, but it might take time even for a rich man to raise that amount of money. No, he would settle for $50,000. The bedroom in his shack had a lock on the door and only a tiny window under the eaves. She could be locked in there until the money was paid. It all seemed so simple. The only problem was that he didn't have a phone, but the woman did, and someone once told him that there was a signal at his shack because it was on a rise.

He had to slow down because the track was very uneven on the slope leading up to his shack. To make matters worse, the woman had become extremely agitated and was fumbling with the door handle. He had to give her a very hard slap to calm her down. But the trickiest part of his plan emerged when they arrived at his shack.

"Stay where you are!" He roared at his captive as he opened the driver's door. His threat had no effect. The woman was out of the car and running back down the track. In his haste, Amos tripped over the trailing remnants of what once had been a seatbelt and ended up sprawled on the stony ground. Howling in pain and rage, he set off after the woman. He was fit from a lifetime of working outdoors and not infrequent flights from the forces of law and order. He caught up with Anoushka before she had run more than a hundred yards.

Manhandling her roughly, he dragged her kicking and screaming towards the shack, cursing as one of her boots briefly found its target. As she attempted another kick, Anoushka lost her balance and stumbled forward. Amos lost his grip but by the time she had regained her balance, he was on top of her, wrenching her arms painfully behind her back. At the entrance to the shack, Amos had to let go of her to insert the key into the lock and Anoushka started hitting him as hard as she could. This resulted in a violent blow to the side of her head, causing a sickening crack. A kaleidoscope of colours whirled before her eyes, then nothing.

She woke up to find herself tied to a chair, with a desperate need to pee. She had no recollection of how she came to be in this place, or of being tied up. Her head was pounding and her left cheek felt on fire. Her wrists and ankles chafed at her bindings, and she was scared—more scared that she would ever have thought possible. What did that dreadful man want with her? The possibilities were the stuff of nightmares.

The room was dark. A faint light filtered through a dirty window near the ceiling, allowing her to take stock of her surroundings. The walls were made of rough wooden planks. The chair to which she was tied, a tin bucket and a filthy mattress on the floor were the only furnishings. The heavy wooden door was closed, and her heart sank as she registered the large metal lock set into it.

She could hear footsteps on the other side of the door and called out, "Let me out! You have no right to keep me here. I need to go to the bathroom. Let me out now, please!"

The sound of footsteps stopped, and she could sense his presence on the other side of the door.

"Let me out!" She yelled.

Silence. Amos was at a loss to know what to do next. It was all proving much more complicated that he had imagined. He would need to untie her hands to allow her to use her phone, and that was likely to result in another barrage of furious fists. And now she wanted to go to the bathroom—not that there was a bathroom in the shack. That was what the bucket was for. But, of course, she couldn't use the bucket if she was tied to the chair, and if he untied her ankles, she would start kicking like a mule again. This was not how it had worked out in the film.

"Stop yelling and let me think."

"There's no time to think if you don't want me to pee all over your chair and floor!"

Anoushka heard his footsteps recede and cried out in desperation. For a few minutes, there was no sound on the other side of the door, then she heard a scraping sound like a stiff cupboard drawer or door being opened, followed by a series of metallic clicks. Amos picked up the revolver he had taken years ago from a man killed in a pub brawl. At the sound of sirens, the man's assailants had made a hasty exit, leaving Amos time to pick up the gun and make his own escape before the police arrived. He had never used it. In fact, he was unsure how it worked. He had tried firing it from the back of the shack soon after he had found it, but it had jammed.

Holding the revolver in his left hand, he unlocked the bedroom door. Anoushka saw the gun and screamed.

"Use the bucket over there!" he said to her as he cut the cords binding her to the chair.

"Too late," she snapped with all the dignity she could muster. The sight of the gun had been enough, and now she was wet through.

"Time to phone your husband or your father," Amos said.

"Why do you want to phone my father?" Anoushka asked, fearing the answer.

"If he wants you back alive, he needs to pay money."

"There's no phone signal in this area."

"Phone signal here—on a hill. Phone your father. I want $50,000."

"$50,000! Are you mad? Who has that kind of money? The best thing would be for you to let me go. My friends will have alerted the police, and they will be searching for me right now. If you let me go, I'll just say that my car broke down and I got lost trying to find my way back. That way, you will stay out of trouble. If you start asking for a ransom for me, you will be in all sorts of difficulty. You'll be facing a very long prison sentence. Just let me go, please."

"Phone your father! $50,000 or I'll kill you!" Amos replied, waving the revolver as he spoke.

"My father's in Istanbul. It's halfway through the night there."

Amos looked blank.

"Istanbul—it's a city in Türkiye."

Amos looked none the wiser. "Phone your father!"

Anoushka took her phone out of her back pocket and, to her surprise, saw that it displayed two bars of signal. Fingers shaking uncontrollably, she dialled a wrong number, cut the call and redialled. At the sound of her father's voice, she burst into tears.

"Anoushka, what's the matter?" Her father was now fully alert.

"Kaçirildim! *I've been kidnapped…*" she started to say.

"Talk English!" Amos barked. "No foreign talk!"

"I'm being held in a shack in the middle of the Australian Outback—after my friends left, I stayed behind to take some photos and my car broke down. This man offered to give me a lift and now he has taken me prisoner, and—"

Amos snatched the phone from her. "$50,000 tomorrow, or the girl dies."

Kadir fought to suppress overwhelming panic and think as a policeman. Trying to keep anger and fear from his voice, he said, "Kidnapping is a very serious offence, Mr... What did you say your name was?"

No response. Amos remembered the kidnappers in the film saying how important it was that no one knew their names.

"Ok. It would be best if you just let Anoushka go, and we can all pretend this didn't happen. We can say that you picked her up and took her back to your home for shelter until help arrived. So, please give her back the phone and let her go."

"$50,000 tomorrow or she dies. Tell him!" he said to Anoushka. "Tell him I have a gun."

"Ok, ok," Kadir replied. "However, I live 13,000 miles away. It's midnight here. I need to get the money and book a flight. I need three days at least."

Amos looked confused.

"My father lives on the other side of the world. It takes 13 hours in an aeroplane to get here," Anoushka tried to explain.

"Two days—no more. Get to Australia. I phone instructions for exchange."

"Adamina kil sağliği yerinde mi?" *Is the man mentally stable?*

"Onun deli olduğunu düşünmüyorum, sadece..." *I don't think he's mad, just...*

"No foreign talk!"

"Sorry, I was just explaining that finding transport out here is very difficult. My father's English is not very good, so sometimes I'll have to speak to him in Turkish if you want him to understand what you want."

Even through the waves of anger and terror, Kadir was impressed by his daughter's presence of mind. Lapsing into Turkish could be very useful.

"How much battery are left?" Kadir asked, to keep up the pretence of poor English. It was doubtful if Amos noticed.

"About half-charged. Sorry Daddy, bina Sydney ile arkeolojik alanin yaklaşik olarak ortasinda yer almaktadir." *The building is about halfway between Sydney and the archaeological site.*

Amos pushed the gun roughly against Anoushka's head.

"My father wanted to know if the battery in my phone would last for two days. Without the phone, you won't be able to give him instructions about where to leave the money."

"Canim, onu konuşturmaya devam et ve telefonunu kapat. Mesajlari control etmek için her iki saatte bir birkaç dakikaliğina tekrar aç." *Keep him talking, darling. Switch off your phone now. Switch it back on for a few minutes every two hours to check for messages.*

"My father says I need to switch off the phone now to save the battery. He can't use a phone while he is travelling, so there is no point in keeping it on. He will contact us when he arrives in Sydney."

Amos snatched the phone from her and Anoushka could have wept. Her chances of checking for messages before tomorrow were gone.

"Food soon," Amos said as he left the room, locking the door behind him.

"Can I have some water, soap and a towel please?"

No answer.

Anoushka had lost track of time, when the door finally opened again and a cracked plate with some greyish meat on it was pushed across the floor. The sight of it turned her stomach. Moments later, a tin cup filled with water arrived. That, at least, she could swallow and was surprised to find that it tasted fresh.

Amos made no attempt to tie her up again, relying on the locked door to keep her imprisoned. As the long, dark hours passed, the temperature in the room dropped and cold air filtered in from somewhere up in the roof. Anoushka's sweat- and urine-soaked clothes clung to her skin, but she didn't dare take them off in case Amos returned. There was no electricity in the shack, but she dreaded asking for an oil lamp or candle, which would probably anger her captor—she had seen the rage that simmered under the surface—nor did she want him entering the room to bring her a light. The less contact she had with Amos, the better. She tried walking backwards and forwards across the narrow space in an attempt to keep warm, but after tripping over the mattress and banging her knee against the chair, she sat down again, shivering from a mixture of cold and fear.

Jens will come for me. Jens will come for me. Jens will come for me—a mantra to supress panic. A mantra to keep a hold on sanity.

Fatigue began to dominate her other discomforts, but the only chair was too hard and unforgiving to allow for sleep. She thought of lying on the floor but quickly rejected that idea as she imagined the frightening variety of insects and small creatures who might share the floor with her. That left the rancid mattress on which she was sure Amos usually slept. She was so tired that she reluctantly decided that the mattress was the least awful option, an option which promised an interminable, restless night.

*

As early-morning light filtered through the grimy window, her eyes flickered open. A pounding head and raging thirst broke through momentary forgetfulness, and she was suddenly fully awake and terrified. This was day two of her captivity and she was losing hope. She could hear no noise coming from the other room in the shack. Where was Amos? Suppose he had taken fright and abandoned her to die in this awful place?

Pull yourself together, Anoushka, you are a Demercol, after all. Your ancestors have fought for survival, fought for victory, and used their wits to get themselves out of tight spots for centuries. Step one is to get yourself off this filthy mattress—oh my God, I smell awful, my clothes smell awful. Well, there is nothing I can do about that right now. Now think—try and charm Amos into letting you out of this room— but what then? The window is too small to squeeze through even if I could reach it. Do I just wait in the hope of being rescued, but how on earth could anyone find this place? When my father phones, should I tell Amos that I can't hear what he is saying and I need to go outside to get a better signal? But what do I do then?

The sound of the door opening broke through the disjointed thoughts racing through her mind. The cracked plate reappeared, unwashed from the night before but bearing what looked like a pancake! The sight of a pancake was so unexpected, so bizarre, that she almost laughed, before grabbing the accompanying cup of water and downing it in one. Moments later, Amos appeared in the doorway, apparently unfazed by the smell. He was holding her phone.

"Your father hasn't called. Does he want you to get killed?"

Anoushka saw the rage rising and tried her best to placate him, "His plane will not have landed yet and you are not allowed to use phones on planes. And even after he lands, he will have to go through immigration and customs, and you can't use a phone there either."

She saw the look of incomprehension on Amos's face and realised that he knew nothing of the trials and tribulations of international travel.

"He will phone later this morning; I am sure of that," she said as softly and reassuringly as she could.

Amos grunted and walked out, slamming the door shut behind him. Anoushka was left shaking. She had seen how close to the edge Amos was.

Jens would come for her, but how? This wasn't one of the cheap romantic novels so loved by her grandmother. Novels in which love bloomed through trials and tribulations and ended happily. Jens did not know where she was, only that she was last seen somewhere in the Australian Outback. Besides, knights on white chargers had not come to the aid of damsels in distress since the time of King Arthur. The police would be looking for her, but where? She was miles from the campsite, and miles from the main road.

The heat and smell in the room were building up to an insufferable level. Anoushka tried the walking-back-and-forth routine in a vain attempt to combat nausea and keep focus, but her legs didn't seem to be working and she collapsed back on the hard seat again.

Pull yourself together and think!

What was the name of the Demercol Grand Vizier who managed to escape from Sultan Murad's dungeons? How had he done it?—can't remember which Sultan Murad it was—there had been so many of them?

She could feel her grasp on reality slipping.

Was that a helicopter she heard—a helicopter in Australia! She laughed out loud, the sound catching in her dry throat, setting off a coughing fit. How many helicopters would be in the sky over the Australian Outback—air ambulances, postal services, police—but how many looking for her? Even if a police helicopter did fly overhead, all the occupants would see was a ramshackle building and a dog. They weren't going to see the little trinket she had dropped as she got out of the car—a trinket only Jens would recognise.

At that moment, Amos came crashing back into the room, phone in hand. "No call from your father! You call him, *now!*"

Anoushka reached out for the phone, but it slipped through her sweat-slick fingers and dropped onto the floor. Amos swore at her. She picked it up, but the screen was blank. She turned the phone on, but the screen remained blank. Fumbling under a barrage of abuse, she tried turning the phone off and on again, to be greeted by a fleeting screen reporting 1% charge before it went blank again.

"Phone him!"

"I can't. It has run out of charge!"

"Run out of what? The signal's good here—on a hill."

"It's not the signal!" She screamed at him. "It's the battery. It's out of charge. You must have left it on all the time.

No wonder you haven't heard from my father. He can't contact you on this. He must be out of his mind with worry."

"Can't you fix it?"

"Not without a charger, and my charger is in my car, five kilometres from where you picked me up. It also needs a power source and there is no electricity in this dump! So, no! I can't fix it."

Amos grabbed the phone, pressing all the controls, finally dropping it on the floor and stamping on it before storming out of the room. Anoushka collapsed onto the chair in floods of tears as she heard the rasping sound of the lock turning.

Baba can't contact me now…

Amos's face was suffused with impotent rage as he guessed what he had done. The night before, he had been transfixed by the screen on the phone, pressing all the little squares one after another. Some wouldn't open. Some just asked him to write something in the blank spaces. Others were full of photographs of strange cities—vast buildings with towering columns around enormous domes; a party with people wearing strange clothes; photos of a man in a pub, the same man in a park, at a table; photos of deserts; and one of a derelict house with lots of workmen in it. Another little square had bus timetables for Sydney in it—then the screen had gone blank and he couldn't get it to light up again. He had forgotten that Anoushka's father had said to keep it switched off, and to switch it back on only for a few minutes every two hours.

He stormed back into the bedroom.

"What have you done, bitch!" He yelled as he struck her hard, sending her flying. He had suddenly decided that it wasn't his fault that the phone wasn't working. She must have done something to it when she dropped it on the floor. He had seen people walking around with phones which were always on. There could only be one reason why this one wasn't working. He stormed back out, slamming the door so hard that the whole shack shook, and the dog started barking.

Chapter 16
The Toxteth Bar, Sydney

Jens was elated when he saw Anoushka's colleagues entering the bar, then worried when he realised that she was not with them. Was she avoiding him? Did she think it was going to be too difficult for her family to accept him?

"Where is Anoushka?" he asked Sam, the research team leader, hoping his voice did not betray the tension he felt.

"Oh, she stayed behind to take some more photographs. You know what she is like when she gets a camera in her hand. We got fed up waiting for her to get back, so left a note to say we were in the Tocky."

"Did no one stay behind with her?" Jens asked, scanning the group and noting to his horror that they were all there.

"Hal offered, but she said she would be right behind us," Sam replied, taking a swift glance at his watch and Jens noticed the flicker of concern as he registered how late Anoushka was.

"Have you tried phoning her?" Jens asked, pulling his phone out of his pocket.

"I did. But the signal comes and goes along that stretch of the road. Goes mostly."

Jen's call went straight through to voicemail. By midnight, he could stand it no longer and even Sam was seriously alarmed.

"We need to go and look for her right now," Jens said.

"We have no vehicles and it will be pitch-black out there—for the first time in weeks, there is high cloud cover."

"What about the vehicles you had earlier?"

"No use, I'm afraid. The SUV belongs to the university, and it is needed by the dean first thing in the morning—after it has been cleaned, of course! The other was hired for the field trip, and we have handed it back."

"Does no one have a car we could borrow?"

"It's not a road for a saloon car. Besides, we have been drinking."

Jens had never felt so sober. By the time Anoushka's colleagues had finished talking about what might have happened to her, he had found the hire company online, booked the SUV out again, but to his frustration could not pick it up until the office opened at 5 am.

Sam looked at him. "You and I should get some sleep if we have to pick up the SUV at dawn."

"Are you coming with me?" Jens asked with barely concealed relief.

"Yes, otherwise you won't know where to look. I'll see you at the hire company at five, unless Anoushka has appeared by then."

Jens lay awake in a turmoil of anxiety. His repeated attempts to call Anoushka continued to go through to voicemail. Sam had told him there was no point in phoning the police until she had been missing for twenty-four hours or more—in other words, not till mid-day. He didn't know that her father was on his second call of the night to the commissioner of New South Wales Police Force while he waited to board a flight at Istanbul International Airport. A senior detective was already questioning Sam at his flat. Helicopters would be out at first light.

"We should probably leave the search up to the police, Jens," Sam said as they met, bleary-eyed, outside the car hire firm shortly before 5 am. "I was interviewed for hours by a detective who was waiting on the doorstep when I got home last night. Seems Anoushka is being held somewhere by a man who gave her a lift. Her father has been in touch with the NSW police and is on his way out here. No one is impressed that we left her on her own."

Jens felt faint. The worst of his waking nightmares had just become reality. "I'm going whether you are or not!"

Wearily, Sam followed Jens into the office of Top Dollar Car Hire—*who thought up these names?* he wondered as Jens submitted his driving licence and credit card to the equally weary-looking customer service officer and signed out a SUV.

Chapter 17
The Search

After leaving the outskirts of Sydney, Jens and Sam drove slowly along the road north, scouring the landscape on either side for any sign of Anoushka or her Toyota. From time to time, they heard the drone of a helicopter overhead. Shortly before mid-day, Sam heard a message arrive on his phone.

"Stop the car, Jens! We have a mobile signal. We may lose it again further on."

Sam studied his phone.

"It's Hal. He says that local radio is reporting that Anoushka's car has been spotted just 200 metres down the steep track from the campsite."

"Anoushka's car, but not Anoushka?"

"No word of her, I'm afraid."

They drove on, reaching the turn-off to the track towards mid-day; only to find the way blocked by a police vehicle. Further up the track, they could see police with sniffer dogs combing the surrounding area. Anoushka's car was being hitched to a large tractor trailer. Jens felt sick. A policeman approached their vehicle.

"What's your interest here, fellas?" The policeman asked none too politely, his eyes searching the interior of the SUV. "Out! Both of you—open all the doors and stand back!"

"My interest is that I am Anoushka Demercol's fiancé and I am out of my mind with worry!" Jens said, more aggressively than intended. He felt Sam place a cautionary hand on his shoulder. Sam knew better than Jens that aggression did not go down well with the Australian police.

Finding nothing suspicious in the SUV, the police ushered Jens and Sam into the back of the police vehicle to answer a few questions, Jens seething with frustration at what he saw as time wasted in the search for Anoushka. *Surely questions could wait till later?*

Sam did his best to minimise confrontation as they answered the predictable questions, "When had each of them last seen Anoushka? Why had she stayed behind after the rest of the research team had left? Why had no one stayed with her—surely they knew the dangers of the Outback? Had the research team seen anyone hanging around the camp or study site in the days before Anoushka disappeared? What had they been doing the day of her disappearance and could anyone corroborate their whereabouts?"

After an interminable fifteen minutes, Sam and Jens were told to be on their way back to Sydney and not to leave the city or their current addresses for the time being. The older policeman placed a hand on Jens' arm as they escorted him back to the SUV. In a surprisingly gentle Scottish accent, he said, "I know you're worried sick, laddie, but go home. Leave the search to the police. We are best equipped to find her for you."

Reluctantly, Jens turned the SUV around and set out on the long drive back to Sydney. They stopped at a layby to eat the tasteless sandwiches Sam had bought from a refrigerated food dispenser at Top Dollar Car Hire. A battered Ute pulled in beside them and a wiry man with weathered skin and a shock of grey hair got out to relieve himself at the side of the road. Jens stepped out into the blistering heat to ask if he had seen a young woman wandering along the road or being picked up by a vehicle the day before.

"That the woman that's gone missing?" The driver asked. "Bad business in this heat. Ain't seen her though—sorry. Might be worth asking old Amos—only guy who lives around these parts. He's a bit simple, but he might have seen something—he's up and down this road a lot doing odd jobs. Hope you find her."

"Where can we find Amos?" Jens asked, aware that he was clutching at straws.

"'Bout 20k further on, you'll see an old post-box at a turn-off to the right. Amos's shack is on a steep rise about 7k up the track. You can't miss it—only building for miles around."

Jens jumped back into the SUV with renewed resolve.

"Has the old boy seen something?" Sam asked.

"No, but he's given me the name of someone who might have done," Jens replied.

Sam groaned inwardly, as he found out that they were about to take a 14k diversion up and down a barely driveable track to ask a man with alleged learning difficulties if he had seen or heard anything about a missing woman. He knew argument would be futile.

*

Jens would not have identified what looked like a rickety birdbox perched precariously on top of a rough wooden pole as a mailbox, but his Australian passenger recognised it immediately for what it was.

Looking at the tyre marks leading off from the main road, Sam said, "Someone skidded off the main road in a mighty hurry, if these tyre marks are anything to go by. Look recent too."

Jens took his word for it, wondering how anyone could tell what was and wasn't recent in this hostile terrain. They proceeded up the track in low gear, dodging the ruts and boulders that littered the way. It seemed to take an interminable time before the land before them began to rise steeply and a single-storey building appeared in the distance.

"That must be it," Jens said, glancing at the odometer, which was registering six kilometres from the turn-off—near enough the seven-kilometre estimate of the Ute driver. He drew to a halt before a sharp bend and went on foot to check the state of the track beyond. What he saw looked more like a narrow riverbed than a road. About halfway up the hill, a beaten-up Ute sheltered from the sun under a crude, wooden canopy. *Utes are obviously the vehicle of choice in this part of the world*, he thought.

Returning to the SUV, he and Sam discussed whether to risk driving onwards, or to play safe and leave the vehicle where it was, half-hidden from the building. They decided to proceed on foot. The main track went no further, so leaving the SUV where it was would not block the way for anyone other than the owner of the building above.

"I think I'll turn the car around while it is still daylight," Jens said. Sam agreed. What neither admitted was a growing sense of unease at what might lie ahead. A four- or five-point turn on uneven ground in failing light would not be conducive to a quick getaway. By now, it was four o' clock in the afternoon but the sun had lost none of its ferocity as it beat down on the scorched hillside. In minutes, the men's light summer clothes were wringing wet, chafing painfully against flesh. Their designer sunglasses were no match for the glare and the barren landscape danced before eyes screwed up to slits in a vain attempt to block out the light. Even the ubiquitous flies had given up for the day.

By tacit agreement, they walked in silence, glancing around anxiously when Sam dislodged a stone which set off a tiny avalanche of its neighbours, the sound reverberating in the silent, oppressive air. They paused at the rickety canopy in the hope of respite from the burning sun, but the sun easily found its way in through the many broken slats. The only possible reason for parking the Ute under the canopy was that the next steep stretch of rubble-strewn track was virtually impassable for any ordinary vehicle.

Sam tried the passenger door, withdrawing his hand quickly from the burning metal. Through the filthy window, he could see drifts of crisp packets, sandwich wrappers, coke cans and cigarette packets. Nothing to indicate that a young woman might recently have been an unwilling passenger. Something on the ground beside the passenger door caught his eye and he bent down to pick it up. Rising slowly, he held it out for Jens to see. They stared in horror at the object, a sense of foreboding gripping both men.

A plastic kangaroo with a joey in its 'jewelled' pouch rolled sightless eyes at the men. They had both been with Anoushka at the Toxteth when she had found the kangaroo in a Christmas cracker, declaring it so magnificently trashy that she had attached it to her camera case as a memento of her time in Australia.

Anoushka had been a passenger in that Ute and had left a cry for help. This was no longer a simple case of asking a local man if he had seen the missing woman on his travels. They were about to confront a man who was holding Anoushka at gunpoint, if local radio reports were to be believed.

"We should call the police," Sam whispered—unsure why he was whispering when no one else was around.

"No signal down here," Jens replied, waving his phone around in frantic circles in a futile attempt to find a single bar on screen.

*

Amos was in a state of mounting confusion and he could feel one of his rages building up. None of this was going to plan, not the way it had worked out in the film. It had slowly dawned on him that he couldn't release the girl once her father had dropped off the ransom money. She knew where he lived, and he had nowhere else to go. The kidnappers in the film had had a helicopter ready to whisk them away to a new life. He could hardly outrun a police car and helicopter in his Ute.

And how would he go about spending $50,000 without raising suspicions when everyone knew he often had to 'borrow' $10 for a beer at the end of an evening? He would have to kill the girl, and he was sorry about that. She had even smiled at him when he undid the ties on her wrists and ankles to allow her to call her father. Women never smiled at him, and he had been almost overwhelmed by the experience. He pushed the thought away. The kidnappers in the film had made a strict rule against liking their victim.

Amos lifted the loose floorboard under which he kept a shotgun—stolen many years ago from a property at which he had been doing some casual labouring. Unlike his old revolver, this gun worked. He had cried when he had had to use it to shoot his last dog. Maybe he would cry when he killed the girl too. That was what killing did to a man.

*

"Do you have a signal on your phone yet, Jens?" Sam asked as they left the canopy.

"No," Jens replied, being careful not to dislodge the kangaroo as he slid his useless phone back into his pocket.

"Neither do I. We're probably too low down still. We might get one at the top, though at the top we'll be in full view of Amos and anyone else who might be in that shack."

"OK. Here's what we'll do," Jens said. "Whoever is in that shack will see us coming up the last stretch of track. It doesn't look like a place that has many visitors, so we may expect a hostile welcome if we both approach from this direction. If you peel off and try to get around to the back of the shack, you might be able to phone for help from there. You might also be able to see inside—see if there is any sign of Anoushka, and whether there is anyone else apart from Amos holding her—and find out if there is a back way into the shack. I'll try playing the innocent and approach by the front door and ask if he has seen Anoushka."

"Jens, he will almost certainly have a gun. This is madness. We should go back to the main road, find a spot with a phone signal and call for help."

"And how long do you think that will take! An hour at least before we can make a call, and God knows how long before the police get here. Can you imagine what he might do to her if he sees the place swarming with police and his hopes of a ransom dashed?"

Relieved that the sun was finally dropping behind a hill, Sam took a wide detour around to the back of the house. Jens waited the agreed 15 minutes, before walking up the track to the front door. A dog chained to a gatepost began to bark at the sound of his approach and the door of the shack burst open to a stream of invective—whether directed at the dog or at Jens was unclear. A large figure stood framed in the doorway. The man's head seemed out of proportion to the powerful body below it and, when he spoke, his voice was unusually light for so big a man.

"What do you want?" was the distinctly unfriendly greeting. "Visitors are not welcome here."

"I am engaged to Miss Demercol, who is with you, I believe. I am very grateful to you for looking after her until I could get here. Goodness knows what would have happened to her if she hadn't found shelter."

"Get back or I'll set the dog on you!"

"No need for that, Sir. I have just come to take Miss Demercol home. I am sure her family will be most appreciative of all you have done for her."

"I don't know what you're talking about. Ain't no one here but me. Now, get out and don't come back."

Out of the corner of his eye, Jens could see Sam at the corner of the shack. Hoping that Amos might turn away, he started as if to go back down the path. Sam gave the thumbs-up, signalling that Anoushka was there, then made a zero with his forefinger and thumb. *So, only Amos holding her.* The next two signs were less encouraging—walking fingers accompanied by a slow shake of the head. *So, no way in from the back.*

Jens turned. At an agreed signal, the two men rushed the front door, catching the receding figure of Amos off-guard, but the much heavier man regained his balance surprisingly quickly and grabbed his shotgun. A museum piece by the look of it, but nonetheless lethal. Sam aimed a wild kick at Amos's elbow and the gun went skittering across the floor. For a moment, all three stood in suspended animation. The rank smell of unwashed man and general filth made the air inside the sweltering shack almost unbreathable.

"Anoushka, it's Jens! Sam and I are here to take you home from where this kind gentlem—"

Before Jens got the last word out, Amos landed a murderous punch on Sam's jaw, sending him reeling backwards, crashing into the door of the room where Anoushka was being held.

"Jens! Thank God it's you! What's going on out there? I'm locked in here."

In the momentary distraction that followed, Jens attempted a low rugby tackle on his much heavier opponent, sending both sprawling on the floor. Amos landed beside his gun, took wild aim and fired. Jens felt a burning pain sear his right shoulder. Anoushka began screaming from behind the locked door. Sam was feigning unconsciousness, waiting for the right moment to break down the door.

Amos was on his feet again, pointing the gun at Jens who was rising slowly from the floor, his left hand clutching his right arm. Amos took aim … and nothing happened. The gun jammed. It had not occurred to Amos that it might need some maintenance if it was to keep functioning over the years since he had taken possession of it. Sam took the opportunity to shoulder the bedroom door, which yielded on his third try, sending him flying into the room to be met by Anoushka's startled face.

"Stay in the room for now," he hissed as Anoushka made for the gap where the door had been. "Until it's safe out there."

Amos threw the gun aside in a rage only for it to go off on its own accord, leaving a neat hole in the wall of the shack. He made for Jens, wild fists beating the injured man onto his knees. Sam jumped on Amos's back trying to pull him off his friend, but it ended up in a three-way tussle. Jens was bleeding badly from his shoulder wound and unable to put up much of a fight and Sam's slight frame was no match against the larger man. A loud crack took them all by surprise, although only momentarily in the case of Amos. Behind him, Anoushka stood, the butt of the old revolver clutched in shaking hands as Amos slid to the floor, blood oozing from a wound on his head.

"Oh my God, have I killed him? I only meant to hit him hard. Was it too hard?"

Jens began to take a professional look at the wound, but Amos was already stirring. Anoushka ran into the bedroom and picked up the ties that had been used on her, and they used them to tie Amos's ankles and hands before he regained full consciousness.

"Let's get out of here before he wakes up and bursts these ties!" Sam yelled as he made for the door, pulling up sharply as he surveyed the scene outside in a mixture of terror and shock. The house was surrounded by heavily armed police. Several police vehicles and an ambulance were parked near the canopy. The armed police had climbed the hill silently on foot.

"Come out! Down on your knees, hands in the air!"

Sam didn't need to be asked twice.

"Who else is in there? Anyone armed?"

Shaking uncontrollably, Sam found his voice. "A kidnapper, my friend Jens and his girlfriend."

"Anyone armed?" The police spokesman barked again.

"The kidnapper has a gun, but I don't think it's working. We've tied him up, but not very well. The girl's ok, but my friend is injured."

"Who are you and why are you here?" The spokesman asked, only slightly less aggressively.

"The girl who was kidnapped is engaged to my friend Jens. We came to search for her. I am Sam Christie, her tutor at Sydney University."

"Big risk for a teacher to take."

"Anoushka went missing from a field trip under my leadership."

"Everyone out, hands in the air!" the spokesman yelled.

Anoushka and Jens came out together, three hands in the air. "He can't put his right arm up," Anoushka shouted. "He's been shot in the shoulder!"

"Where's the other guy?"

A furious roar came from inside the shack and four armed officers moved in, weapons raised. A few minutes later, Amos was brought out, securely handcuffed to an equally large policeman.

Meanwhile, three plainclothes police officers approached the terrified friends, separated them and began questioning them. Anoushka broke down as the sympathetic woman police officer asked about her kidnapping. She couldn't take any more and moved towards Jens, who was still being questioned. He turned towards her and put his good arm around her shoulders.

"Surely this can wait until we have got Anoushka home, Officer," he said brusquely. The officer acquiesced.

"How did you find us?" Sam asked after initial questioning was over.

"We weren't looking for you, or your friend. We had rough coordinates from the second phone call the girl made to her father. The helicopter pilot noticed some unusual activity around the shack—a new van parked at the end of the track and two men climbing the hill. We thought the owner of the shack might have kidnapped the girl to order from someone who knew who her father is. He is down there, waiting very impatiently, incidentally."

Kadir watched in an agony of frustration as the figures around the shack began to move down the hillside. A bruised and battered Sam led the way, talking to an accompanying officer. Behind them, a slight woman stumbled over the rough ground supported by a man, a policewoman walking alongside. Last came a great bear of a man handcuffed to two policemen with a further two armed officers keeping a very close guard on the captive.

As the group came nearer, a red mist descended on Kadir as his ultimate nightmare appeared to play out before his eyes. The man clutching his daughter was von Seidel's son! Had he traced her all the way to Australia and kidnapped her in revenge for the arrest and imprisonment of his father? Kadir tried to step over the police cordon but was held back by a very firm hand.

"You must leave this to us, Sir. You'll see your daughter soon enough."

The sharp command was enough to clear the red mist and Kadir looked up the hill again with a policeman's more objective eye. Timmerman's left arm was around his daughter's waist, her head resting on his left shoulder. A large red stain spread across Timmerman's right shoulder and chest. Despite the pain he must have been suffering, Kadir watched as he raised his left arm over Anoushka's shoulder to move back some hair that was sticking to her face. The gentle touch of a lover, not the action of a kidnapper. The kidnapper in question was giving his police escorts a hard time, cursing and swearing as they wrestled him down the hill.

Jens saw Kadir seconds before Anoushka did. They hesitated momentarily, Jens slowly releasing her until Anoushka resolutely placed her head back on his shoulder. This was not how they had envisaged telling her father about their relationship, but it was done now. That hurdle was over and they would simply have to face her parents' reaction together.

The police cordon was lifted to allow Anoushka, Jens and Sam to walk towards the waiting paramedics at the ambulance. Sam's cuts and rapidly developing bruises were swiftly dealt with. Anoushka was severely dehydrated and put on a drip inside the ambulance. It was too early to say what further care might be needed to help her come to terms with her ordeal, but her screams when paramedics tried to move Jens away to look at his shoulder told their own story. A commotion broke out near the canopy. Kadir had broken free from his police 'minder' and was running towards the ambulance. Before anyone could stop him, he had pushed past the paramedic patching up Jens' shoulder and jumped into the ambulance, grabbing his daughter in such a tight embrace that he nearly dislodged her drip. He couldn't speak, tears streaming down his face.

"Shh, Babaciğim. I'm ok. It was all my silly fault. I should not have stayed behind on my own. Thankfully, Jens and Sam came for me. I'm not harmed. I'm ok. I'm so sorry to have put you and Mumya through this. Shh, shh."

"You'll need to come away now, Sir," a police officer said, not unkindly. "The ambulance needs to be on its way—your daughter needs to be checked out and her young man will need surgery on that shoulder according to the paramedics.

"I'm going nowhere!"

"I'm sorry, Sir, but you can't accompany her in the ambulance. We'll take you back to Sydney along with Sam Christie, who is in no fit state to drive."

"Where is the man who kidnapped my daughter?" Kadir asked angrily.

"He has already left in a police van accompanied by four particularly unsympathetic armed officers. He won't be seeing his 'country estate' again for a very long time!"

Reluctantly, Kadir allowed himself to be ushered out of the ambulance into a waiting police car.

"I'll be ok, Baba," Anoushka called after him. "Jens is with me."

She had no idea of the impact these few words had on her already traumatised father.

Chapter 18
The Shangri-La Hotel, Sydney
Twenty-Four Hours Later

Anya and John Arbuthnot were in the lounge bar of the Shangri-La Hotel, gazing out over the magnificent panorama of Sydney Harbour. They had arrived thirty-six hours earlier to support Kadir and Ayşe through the worst nightmare of their lives. While the NSW police commissioner had given permission for Kadir to accompany the police search, he had adamantly refused to allow Ayşe or John to go too.

The initial overwhelming relief at Anoushka's escape had given way to new tensions. Kadir and Ayşe had collected Anoushka from hospital the previous evening and brought her back to the Shangri-La. Jens was being kept in hospital for a further night. Over dinner, Kadir had been unable to keep his fears at bay. Anoushka had managed to maintain a respectful silence while her father expounded on the unsuitability of the work she was doing and the unnecessary risks she had taken, but when he began asking what she really knew about Jens Timmerman, Anoushka had left the table abruptly and stormed off to her room.

She left the hotel early next morning to return to her lodgings for fresh clothes before heading off to the hospital to see Jens. She phoned her mother later to say that Jens had been discharged and that they were on their way to the airport to meet Jens's parents—his *real* parents—arriving from Buenos Aires. The inflexion in Anoushka's voice was not lost on her mother.

"We'll meet you at the hotel bar at six-thirty this evening, if that's ok with you. Jens's parents and sister will join us shortly afterwards."

"That will be lovely, dear. Don't be cross with your father. Last night, he was just releasing the tension of the last few days. I'll make sure he is on his best behaviour tonight."

"Make sure you do, please, Mumya. Love you."

"Love you too. We both do."

Accompanied by a suitably chastened Kadir, Ayşe joined the Arbuthnots in the hotel bar just before 6 pm. *I think I need a stiff drink to face whatever comes next,* Ayşe thought. *Anoushka and Kadir are so alike. When tensions are running high, it only takes a single wrong word from either of them for reconciliation to turn into revolution.* At what point had their happy-go-lucky youngest child changed into this determined young woman? Australia had changed her. Jens Timmerman had changed her and Kadir would just have to get over it.

Two beautifully dressed young people had entered the bar, looking around for familiar faces. They were walking hand-in-hand, the man's right arm encased in a heavy sling. They bore so little resemblance to the battered, dishevelled couple Kadir had seen the day before that it took him a moment to realise who they were as they approached.

Ayşe was already on her feet. Anya stifled a gasp as she looked at Jens—the facial similarity to a man who, years earlier, had tried to kill her was profoundly shocking. As she rose to her feet, she felt John's comforting hand grip hers—he too had almost lost his life at the hands of Hans Peter von Seidel. Introductions were made, accompanied by stiff handshakes, then everyone sat down. An awkward silence fell on the group.

"Can I get you something to drink?" John asked the young couple.

"Perhaps later," Jens replied, taking a deep breath before launching into a brief speech he had obviously been thinking about all day.

"I know I am in the company of three people who encountered Hans Peter von Seidel in the worst possible circumstances; and one person who did not actually meet him but lived through the trauma of those times. Sadly, I cannot do anything about my physical resemblance to the von Seidels, but I am not that man. He was *not* my father. *My father* will arrive shortly with my mother and sister. He is Jan-Marten Timmerman, the father who, from the day I was born, has cared for me, taught me right from wrong and made me the person I am. I owe him and my mother everything I have become.

"Anoushka and I met by chance here in Sydney. We had known each other for several months—long enough to fall in love—before we discovered the link between my genetic heritage and the awful events that took place in Istanbul in 1995. Anoushka and I have come to terms with that, and we love each other. That is all I shall say for the moment. I know this is difficult news for everyone to hear—for all sorts of reasons, not least geographical ones—but we hope you can come to accept the situation in time."

Anoushka turned towards him and smiled, gripping his hand until a sharp intake of breath alerted her to the fact that the hand she was gripping was at the end of a sling. Her stricken look and abject apology broke the tension in the room.

Moments later, a tall, silver-haired man with grey-blue eyes arrived at the table. To his side, a beautiful, dark-haired woman stood surveying the group, a distinct challenge in her eyes and the set of her mouth. Maria-Silvia—ready to defend her son at the slightest provocation. By contrast, the slight young woman behind her had eyes only for Jens.

"I am Jens's father," Jan-Marten announced, a broad smile disguising the anxiety he felt for his son. As the others rose to their feet, Anya and Ayşe noticed the worried look passing from Grazia to Jens—a wordless "is everything ok?" look from a fond sister to her brother. A good sign.

Greeting the Demercols, Jan-Marten said, "My son has told me how well you looked after him and his friend, Federico, when they were in Istanbul. I can't thank you enough and I hope we can return the hospitality one day soon."

Was it Jan-Marten's unforced grace and good humour or Maria-Silvia and Grazia's obvious delight in being with Jens that changed the evening for everyone. Jens and Anoushka took the visitors across to the window to point out the Opera House, the Harbour Bridge and Botanic Gardens thirty-six floors below. Maria-Silvia and Grazia were intrigued by the ferries plying their way back and forth across the harbour, taking their cargos of tired commuters, sunburnt tourists and fare-dodging seagulls to their destination of choice.

Inevitably, talk turned to the events of the past few days and, unprompted, Kadir thanked Jens warmly for rescuing his daughter.

"Isn't it amazing?" Jan-Marten mused. "Just when you think your children have reached a stage when they can't surprise you anymore, they do!"

"I don't know about anyone else, but all this excitement is making me hungry," John announced. "Should we see if this fine establishment can provide us with anything to eat?"

At the sound of these words, a waiter appeared from nowhere, clutching menus.

Later, as they got ready for bed, John turned to Anya. "Did you notice a strange thing that happened this evening?"

"Just about everything that happened this evening was strange," she replied.

"What I noticed, as the evening wore on, was that Jens ceased to remind me of Hans Peter—his voice, his mannerisms, his laugh are so like Jan-Marten's. He is Jan-Marten's son in every way that matters. I hope Kadir can see that."

"I hope Kadir can see that he was also brought up by a very fine mother who had her own terrifying history with Hans Peter. If she can close her mind to the physical similarity between her son and her tormentor, surely the rest of us can. My real concern for Kadir and Ayşe is that if Jens's and Anoushka's relationship survives, Anoushka will probably end up living in Argentina or Australia."

"More travel for all of us then, Anya. We have never been to Argentina."

Chapter 19
Aftermath

Three couples were relaxing with friends over coffee and drinks on the deck of a seafood restaurant at the waterfront in Manly—the tensions of the last few days replaced by growing trust. Jens and Anoushka had left to go for a walk along the shore, Maria-Silvia's anxious plea not to overexert themselves left hanging in the air.

"What an unbelievable sequence of events brought us together to enjoy this beautiful place," Jan-Marten mused.

"Here we are: three couples from three continents separated by thousands of miles of water, different languages and different cultures, enjoying the late afternoon sunshine on a fourth continent. And four different versions of English being spoken around this table. American English—Argentina-style; pure Oxford English—Demercol-style; Welsh English from Anya; and Scottish English from John! To say nothing of the Australian English all around us. It's enough to scramble anyone's language receptors."

"Of course, Kadir and Ayşe are used to living in a latter-day Tower of Babel and have to move from one continent to another on a daily basis," John added. Maria-Silvia gave him a puzzled look.

"What my silly friend means," Kadir replied, "is that Istanbul straddles two continents, Europe and Asia. All you need to do is cross a short bridge to move from one to the other without noticing the join."

"I didn't know that. Is it not rather confusing?"

"Not really. Istanbul is a very old city and the borders of the country we now know as Türkiye have shifted so much over time that Istanbulüs have become used to living with complexity. The land has been ruled by Greeks, Persians, Romans, Byzantines, Seljuk Turks and Ottomans. Phoenicians, Assyrians, Mongols and Russians have invaded parts of the territory over the centuries.

"It is the fault of our otherwise beautiful location. Whoever controls Istanbul controls the Dardanelles, the Bosphorus and the navigation route between the Mediterranean and the Black Sea. A power base for whoever wants to keep the Russian bear at bay, and their hands on the lucrative trade from East to West. No wonder our youngest daughter has chosen to do her anthropological research in Australia. Where would you begin, in Türkiye?"

Conversation drifted across the world to Sydney and its breathtakingly beautiful harbour.

The Timmermans were enthusing about the ferry journey from Circular Quay to Manly, an experience everyone had enjoyed—old Sydney hands vying with each other to point out landmarks on the way. Jan-Marten suddenly stopped mid-sentence as John leapt to his feet, sending his chair crashing to the ground.

"John, are you alright? You look as if you have seen a ghost!"

John was on the move, taking the steps down from the restaurant to the roadside two at a time. He began to run, then gave up, standing stock-still looking for something, or someone, amid the throng of beachgoers heading home.

Returning breathless to the table, he announced to his bewildered friends, "I have just seen Ronnie Manson walking past! Ronnie Manson is supposed to be dead—killed when his car went up in flames. But it was him! I am absolutely certain."

"Ronnie Manson!" Kadir exclaimed, jumping to his feet and following John back to the roadside.

Anya and Ayşe let out a collective groan. The Timmermans looked startled.

*

"I guess we had better head back—our parents' stress levels have been sorely tested these last few days. My mother will already be thinking we have fallen off a cliff into the Atlantic while being devoured by a snake." As they made their way back along the cliff path, Jens and Anoushka noticed two birdwatchers gazing fixedly out to sea through very professional-looking binoculars.

"I wonder what they have seen," Anoushka said.

"I wonder what they do on the other six days of the week," Jens replied, only to be rewarded by a puzzled glance.

"What do you mean?"

"Look at what's written on the back of their T-shirts. *Sunday Scientists. Sydney 2015.*"

Anoushka laughed. "It's probably a birdwatching club or society."

Back on the beach road, they stepped out of the way as four cyclists rode past, all wearing similar T-shirts.

"Birdwatching from the saddle of a bike can't be easy." Jens laughed. "Back to my earlier question—what do the *Sunday Scientists* do on the other six days of the week?"

Suddenly, up ahead, all was confusion as a pedestrian ran out in front of the bikes, causing a collision as the leading riders swerved abruptly to avoid knocking the man down. One of the cyclists got up quickly, but the other was trapped under her bike. Jens set off at a run to attend to the woman as the other cyclists stood around her protectively. She was feeling dizzy but thankful for the helmet which had absorbed most of the blow as she hit the kerb. A nasty cut on her wrist where it had caught the pedal was bleeding profusely. She looked up as a passer-by with a gentle voice dropped to his knees beside her.

"I'm Jens," he said. "I'm a doctor. Would you like me to have a look at that cut?"

"I'm Angie," she replied. "Yes please—I'm feeling a bit wobbly, to tell the truth."

"I'm not surprised—what an irresponsible idiot that guy was."

Two of the cyclists lifted Angie's bike off her legs while Jens and Morag, one of the other cyclists, helped her onto a chair brought out from the restaurant.

Before removing her helmet, Jens asked Angie if she felt sick, had blurred vision, a headache or ringing in her ears. Satisfied with the answers, he proceeded to dress the cut as best he could with the first-aid pack from her saddlebag but advised her to get it stitched and dressed properly at a medical centre. By this time, John and Kadir had joined the group of spectators, alerted by the confusion.

A surfer approached one of the cyclists, phone in hand.

"I got a video shot of the dumb ass who ran out in front of your friends," he said. "If you give me your number, I'll forward it to you."

"Thanks. I'm Stuart. A photo would be great, but I'm not sure the police will be all that interested as no one was seriously injured."

"The police may not be," the surfer replied, pointing to the badly buckled wheel on Angie's bike, "but the bike hire company almost certainly will be!"

John overheard the exchange. "Let me see that photo."

"Sure, mate," said the surfer, slightly taken aback at the abrupt tone of voice.

"It's him, Kadir! It's him! And he is looking over his shoulder to see if anyone is following. There is a clear image of his face. He must have recognised one of us and legged it."

"Belatedly remembering his manners, John explained to the astonished surfer and cyclists that the man was wanted by the police in several countries; he asked if the surfer would forward the photo to him."

Aware that it was only 5.30 am at police headquarters in Glasgow, John phoned the duty officer and told him to call the superintendent as early as he dared. He was in possession of a photograph which proved that a Scottish child-trafficker, drug dealer and murderer was not as dead as everyone had been led to believe; that the charred remains found in that individual's burnt-out car belonged to someone else. Someone who presumably had not volunteered for the role of Ronnie Manson lookalike.

*

Angie and Morag set off by taxi to the nearest Medicare Clinic, promising to be back as soon as possible. John and Kadir returned to face the inevitable tirade from their wives. Their assurance that any involvement in a Ronnie Manson hunt would go no further than a phone call to Police Scotland was met with more than a little scepticism.

"You look puzzled, Kadir."

"Didn't the Scottish police carry out forensic tests on the remains found in Ronnie Manson's car?"

"They didn't see the need. Reg Manson confirmed that Ronnie had left home alone, driving that car; the burnt-out car had been on the route Reg said Ronnie was taking; the charred remains of clothing found in a case in the boot of the car were allegedly Ronnie's, as was what was left of an Omega watch. The police would have seen little point in wasting scarce resources on further testing.

"No one had witnessed the accident. There was no evidence of any other vehicle being involved. Reggie had no desire to see the case investigated further and, as far as the police were concerned, one Manson fewer on the streets of Glasgow had to be good news. Case closed."

"What's this about?" Jan-Marten asked.

"The Mansons are a gangland family in Glasgow. Ronnie Manson was wanted on a charge of child trafficking when he allegedly died in a blazing car," John explained. "Somebody died in that car, but it looks as if that person wasn't Ronnie. That's why I must talk to Police Scotland."

"Can't you find anything more interesting to talk about when we are sitting in a wonderful restaurant in Manly, John?

You are retired, and we are on holiday. Phone Police Scotland if you must, but you are not to start combing the streets of Sydney looking for a phantom! We all have a double somewhere and that is almost certainly what you saw. Let it drop."

At that moment, a tall, dark-haired man accompanied by an entourage of people wearing T-shirts emblazoned with *Sunday Scientists. Sydney 2015* entered the restaurant. To break the tension at his own table, Jens set off to solve the mystery of what these people did on the other six days of the week.

"Science—for at least half of our group. I'm Jack. And you are?"

"Jens. Jens Timmerman."

Smiling broadly at the younger man's curiosity, Jack continued, "We have zoologists, ornithologists, chemists, biologists and physicists in our ranks, but we have diversified with partners and friends from many different disciplines—it keeps us from talking science all the time. We meet quarterly for lunch on a Sunday—hence the name, *Sunday Scientists.*"

An attractive woman holding a glass rather precariously whispered something in Jack's ear. "Thanks, Isobel," he whispered back.

"Are you the doctor who helped Angie?"

"Yes," Jens replied, colouring slightly.

"We cannot thank you enough," Isobel said. "Can we offer drinks for your table?"

"Absolutely no need. For once, I just happened to be at the right place at the right time."

"And now, you must tell us about *your* interesting table," Stuart said.

"Where to start! Our table comprises a former police superintendent from Scotland; a commander with the Istanbul police; a lawyer, doctor and Jesuit priest from Argentina; an anthropologist from Istanbul; a retired UK diplomat; two laboratory technicians from a kidney research centre in Argentina; the founder and manager of a soup kitchen in Istanbul; and one genuine Australian academic. If you would like to find out how all this fits together, you will have to join us for drinks after your meal."

"We should do that. It sounds as if there is a fascinating story there, and one of our Sunday Scientists writes fiction. This could prove to be the inspiration for her next novel!"